IN ECSTASY

IN ECSTASY

KATE McCAFFREY

annick press
toronto + new york + vancouver

© 2009 Kate McCaffrey

Annick Press Ltd.
All rights reserved. No part of this work covered by the copyrights
hereon may be reproduced or used in any form or by any means—
graphic, electronic, or mechanical—without prior written permission
of the publisher.

First published in 2008 by Fremantle Press, Freemantle, Australia

This edition copy edited by Heather Sangster
This edition proofread by Tanya Trafford
Cover design by Black Eye Design

Cataloging in Publication

McCaffrey, Kate, 1970-
        In ecstasy / Kate McCaffrey.

ISBN 978-1-55451-175-4 (bound).—ISBN 978-1-55451-174-7 (pbk.)

        1. Ecstasy (Drug)—Juvenile fiction. 2. Drug addiction—Juvenile
fiction.
3. Peer pressure—Juvenile fiction. I. Title.

PZ7.M135In 2009   j823'.92   C2008-907665-6

Printed and bound in Canada

Distributed in Canada by   Published in the U.S.A. by
Firefly Books Ltd.   Annick Press (U.S.) Ltd.
66 Leek Crescent   Distributed in the U.S.A. by
Richmond Hill, ON   Firefly Books (U.S.) Inc.
L4B 1H1   P.O. Box 1338 Ellicott Station
                                  Buffalo, NY 14205

Visit our website at www.annickpress.com
Visit Kate McCaffrey at www.katemccaffrey.com

For Jase

sophie

Mia and I had never been in the shop before—it was one of those places you just passed by. We knew there was nothing either of us could afford: they had the kind of stuff you saw in the magazines my mom bought, with price tags in the thousands. Inside, dresses arranged by color hung on iron rods suspended from the ceiling by invisible wires. It was supposed to look classy, but to me it was contrived and pretentious.

"Well?" She looked at me expectantly.

I watched people entering and leaving through a timber-paneled arched doorway—attracted, no doubt, by the tiny SALE sign stuck to the front window. It was weird, but I was nervous. I always was. We were shoppers, we had money—nowhere near enough, but it wasn't against the law to browse. They couldn't arrest us for looking, could they? Really though, it had nothing to do with any of that. It was because I knew we were going in to do the wrong thing.

"Yeah," I said, smiling to hide my nervousness, "but remember, you have to try on whatever I give you."

She grinned wickedly. "And that goes for you too."

Mia headed straight for the rack of orange. Bitch, I thought, until my eyes landed on the purples. I walked past the shop assistants without making eye contact. I figured if I acted like I had every right to be there nobody would say a word.

"Soph, I've found it," Mia shouted. "It'll go perfect with your pointy-toed, red patent stilettos." The shoes were fictitious of course; this was just Mia's attempt at embarrassing me totally. In her hand hung an orange dress that I wouldn't be caught dead in.

"Yeah, beautiful," I said, thrusting a mauve-and-yellow paisley at her, "and isn't this *exactly* the dress you fell in love with in *Vogue*?"

One of the assistants was trying not to hover, and I couldn't help feeling sorry for her. Mia watched her with barely hidden delight. This was part of the dare too— not just who could embarrass the other the most but who could make the biggest impact. In this respect, Mia usually outperformed me.

Flicking the tag on the orange dress made me gasp. Some sale! No wonder the assistant was trying not to have a heart attack. At half-price it was still thirteen hundred dollars. That was as much as my brother's car!

The brocade curtain swung on its wrought-iron rod as I slid out of my jeans and T-shirt and wriggled into the dress.

"Is it on?" Mia shouted from behind the other curtain, another of her strategies. Usually she's quite soft-spoken.

I stifled my laughter. "Yep, it's gorgeous. What about you?"

"Oh yeah, you're gonna die."

I ripped open my curtain at the same time she whipped hers back.

"Oh my God, Sophie," Mia exclaimed, so loudly all heads in the shop turned our way. "You look like Barbie."

I looked at my reflection. The dress had given me cartoonlike proportions—my boobs jutted out like pointy cones and the dress hugged me tightly around the waist.

Mia pretended to sound concerned. "Soph, are you all right? Oh my God, can you breathe?"

I couldn't, because I was laughing so hard. The shiny satin of the paisley dress stopped above her knees, and she'd left her boots on and hauled her socks up. The dress was the ugliest thing I'd ever seen in my life. I lost it. I hung on to the curtain laughing so hard I thought I'd split the dress. But Mia wasn't finished.

"Good God, girl, you're a danger to society," she said. "You could take someone's eye out with those."

"And you look like someone's grandma on acid," I shot back.

We clutched each other, laughing hysterically.

"They're weapons of mass destruction."

"Shut up," I choked.

"So, girls, how are you doing for sizes?" The assistant's face was clear—she wanted us out.

"Fine," I said, trying to compose myself.

"Just perfect," Mia said, and I don't know how she does it, but she went from laughter to serious in the blink of an eye. "So, Sophie, what do you think? Would you wear it to the party tonight?"

"Hmm." I rubbed my chin. "It would go with the shoes, but maybe it's too dressy?"

"We'll think about it," Mia said, going back into her changeroom.

Mia figured I'd won that one, but I didn't agree. I could've peed my pants—probably would have if I hadn't been wearing orange silk. I could just imagine the sales woman pointing to a sign—"If you pee in it, you pay for it."

We ended up finding some great clothes on sale, real clothes that normal people can afford. And it was fun getting ready for Dom's party, even though every time I thought about seeing him I felt like throwing up. But Mia was so excited. And when she was dressed, and had made me re-do her hair fifty times, she looked amazing. She knew it too. I could tell by the way she smiled to herself. It was hard not to let her excitement infect me. By the time we walked out the front door of my house, I couldn't wait to get there either.

mia

The music penetrated my shoulder blades through the wall I was leaning against. It was Tegan & Sara, so loud it was vibrating my skull. I couldn't understand the attraction. I just didn't get it. Other girls closed their eyes against the beat and snapped to its rhythm. I closed my eyes too–the pain in my temple was piercing and my heels were raw where my new shoes rubbed.

Where was Sophie? I was fed up and tired. My confidence had evaporated. Soph was my lifeline, and she'd vanished. How could she? She knew I was lost without her. We were only here because it was her ex's birthday. Dominic Cimino is totally gorgeous, a genuine grade twelve centerfold with a pulse. I think I was more heartbroken than Sophie when she split up with him.

Soph is that girl. In grade ten, she was the girl who always went out with grade eleven and twelve guys. She's the chick you see in the cafeteria talking to guys you'd love to talk to but don't because they have no idea who you are. Next to Soph, most girls feel pretty insignificant. She's outgoing and self-confident. Her sideways, under-the-eyebrow look is a killer. The captain of the football team dumped his girlfriend for Soph after that look. Everyone in school knows her. And she's the girl with the quiet friend who tags along behind. Yeah, that's me. It's only through Sophie that I have any social life at all. Thank God she's my best friend.

I'd been so excited about going to a real party. No parents, and total freedom to do what I liked. Soph and I had hit the stores and I came home with the boho look–a turquoise and brown flowing top over vintage denim jeans. The shoes, which were now causing me extreme agony, were the finishing touch: a lethal stiletto, also in turquoise. I felt like I'd stepped straight off the pages of *Seventeen*. I was bursting with self-confidence.

The minute we arrived, however, it was another matter. I stood slightly behind Sophie on the sidewalk, clutching a pack of vodka coolers. The entrance was down the side of the house, a narrow alleyway decorated with party lights. The music was loud from the street, and the closer we got, the harder the beat invaded our bodies. The backyard was bursting with people. Many of them I recognized from school, but they seemed so much older here. I felt pretty intimidated. Everyone was dancing and drinking. I looked at Soph, waiting for instructions. I didn't know what to do. She'd been to plenty of parties like this, as someone's girlfriend.

"Have a drink," she said, pulling a bottle from its cardboard packaging.

I took it from her, the wet sides slipping in my hand, and twisted it open. I watched Soph survey the crowd as we both chugged our drinks. I belched loudly and then covered my mouth, embarrassed.

"What do you say?" she asked in her best parental voice.

"Good one," I said loudly, and we both laughed. I felt myself beginning to relax. Maybe the vodka was working already. We both took another one and shoved the rest of the bottles into a bin full of ice and drinks.

"Come on," Sophie said, leading the way into the crowd. I took a deep breath and followed. She made a beeline for Dominic, like a girl on a mission. He was in the games room, standing with his new girlfriend and some friends. It was like hot guy central there. Karen Baxter, the girlfriend, is in grade twelve and president of the student council. She's pretty in an understated way–clear skin, perfectly symmetrical face. She's the type of girl who can get away with wearing no makeup, and her hair is ramrod straight. I watched her face tighten as Soph approached Dominic and kissed him on the cheek, laughing flirtatiously and wishing him happy birthday. He left his hand too long around her waist. Both Karen and I saw it. Dominic still had the hots for Sophie.

Karen leaned in and put her hand on Dominic's arm. "I need a drink," she said.

He gave her a smile. "Me too," he said. "Will you get me one while you're at it?" He looked at Soph and then at me. "What about you two, need a drink?"

We both shook our heads and I watched Karen slink off like a kicked dog. Soph acted like she was oblivious to the power she wielded, and I stood silently behind her, watching Dominic fall for her all over again.

Where was she? I stood in the games room, watching everyone dancing and laughing in a sea of white smiley teeth. I was shifting my weight from one foot to the other and finally just had to slide the shoe off the back of my left foot.

9

It was burning hot, and already a blister was forming in the red rawness. I was all alone, drinking rum and Coke out of a plastic cup. Somebody had taken our drinks, so I'd stolen someone else's. I figured that was the way it went.

I was watching Karen out in the garden. As the night progressed she'd drunk herself stupid. Now she was fertilizing the rose bushes, staggering and holding on to a thorny branch, her long legs pointed inwards at the knees as she swayed and puked. Dominic was nowhere in sight.

"Hey, look who I've found," Sophie shouted in my ear. Finally, she was back. I turned around and nearly dropped dead. She was hanging on to Lewis Scott's arm.

Lewis Scott is a dream god, and I'm not alone in my fantasies about him. His name has been scrawled on bathroom walls by hundreds of girls, me included. But now it seemed like Soph had him under her spell, so I'd probably get to know him by default.

"Hi," I said, smiling and jamming my heel back into my shoe.

"Having a good time?" he asked.

"Fantastic," I lied, my stomach flipping out from looking up at him. Lewis has to be well over six feet tall—he towered over both Soph and me. He has spiky blond hair and blue eyes. He's the type of guy you'd expect to see in

Cosmo. He is absolute sex on legs.

"Where've you been, Soph?" I tried not to sound too pissed off.

She ignored my question. "Lewis has got something for us," she said, nudging him flirtatiously and giving him that look. "Go on, Lewis, show her."

Lewis dug into his pocket and looked at Sophie. She nodded her head, laughing coyly. His blue eyes pierced mine as, like a magician, he offered me his fist.

"What?" I asked, trying to get into their light-hearted mood.

He turned his fist over and opened his fingers. In the middle of his palm sat three small round yellow pills. They weren't smooth and perfectly formed like normal pills; the edges were rough and fibrous. And faintly in the middle of each was the imprint of a tiny butterfly.

"Shall we?" Sophie shouted in my ear. "It's an E." She was smiling and nodding her head. Lewis was also smiling. Everyone was smiling but me. I wanted to be smiling too.

"Okay," I said. I took one out of his hand and put it straight into my mouth, washing it down with the flat rum and Coke. I looked at them both like it was no big deal, but internally I stressed about what might happen. Sophie was watching me expectantly.

"It'll take about twenty minutes," Lewis said as he handed one to Sophie and threw the last one into his mouth.

Thirty minutes later nothing had happened. Sophie saw Dominic go by looking pretty upset and ran outside after him, leaving me alone with Lewis.

"What's up with them?" he asked me.

I shrugged my shoulders. I wanted to say something really clever, something to make him interested in me. "Dunno."

"Isn't he with Karen?"

I nodded, resigned to the fact that he wanted to talk about Soph. It was always Sophie. Guys only talked to me because of her. I was a nobody. I tried to think of things to talk to him about.

"Great party," I offered lamely.

"Yeah," he agreed, looking off into the crowd, watching the dancers. I stood awkwardly beside him, trying not to move in case I dislodged the thin piece of skin covering my throbbing heel. Outside, Karen was asleep under the rosebush, her white capri pants a mess of puke and grass stains. Not far from her, Soph and Dominic stood together. Soph had a hand on his arm, looking up at him, talking softly.

Lewis hung around for all of five minutes, shifting awkwardly beside me, then said he had to go and see someone. I watched him walk off. Immediately he seemed to move more freely and started laughing with some of his friends. I was totally cut. I didn't fit in. All the effort I'd put into getting ready had been a waste of time. All my expectations were just wishful thinking. I should've stayed home. I was a total loser.

I went to find Soph. She and Dom were no longer in the garden. The music had got louder and my mood worse. The diehard dancers were still at it, covered in sweat, their faces red and shiny. Nobody looked at me as I slid through the crowd, invisible.

Then I saw her, sitting on the floor next to Craig, which was really weird. Craig's in our class at school and has a reputation for violence—once he ended up doing time in a juvenile detention center. I've never had anything much to do with him, but he was sitting pretty close to Soph, and they were obviously having some kind of deep and meaningful conversation. I didn't want to break into it, but I had to tell her I was going home.

"Soph," I said softly. Both she and Craig smiled up at me. Even Craig had a warm, friendly smile. It freaked me out.

"Mia. You look so beautiful," she said, reaching up to

touch my face. And then I felt it kick in. I was suddenly awash with the most peaceful, tranquil feeling. Her fingers stroked every molecule in my skin. Her touch was like a hundred butterflies fluttering across my face.

"God, Soph, that's amazing." I dropped from my crouch into a sitting position next to her. Craig was watching, smiling benignly. I started touching her face like I was a blind person. The contact of her skin against my fingers thrilled me. It was all-consuming. I leaned back against the wall; the rough bricks penetrated my top and prickled my spine in an exquisite way. I moved forward and backward, and the texture rushed through my veins. Wherever my body made contact with another object–the wall, the floor, Sophie, my own clothes–I was saturated by these intense sensations. I'd been so down only seconds before, but Sophie's touch had turned that all around.

I leaned against the wall thinking how much I loved her. I watched the beautiful people around me moving to the beat. I heard the pulse of the universe. Suddenly I understood why we existed. Every breath I took moved the air around me. Atoms and molecules parted as my mouth drew in a wake of air. I watched myself exhale the particles. I reached up and touched them, floating around me.

All my senses were magnified. The lights were vivid, and

they streaked as I turned my head. The music was beautiful; it became part of my rhythm, it spoke to me in a way music never had before. It had been like a foreign language, but all of a sudden I understood what it meant. I closed my eyes and absorbed the beat.

I felt a hand on my leg. I opened my eyes and Lewis was sitting on the floor next to me, smiling at me. He was so beautiful. His hand was heavy on my thigh, sending electric shocks up my body. I put my hand on top of his and laced my fingers through his. Then I reached up and touched his face. As I made contact with his skin I realized how much I loved him. I'd always watched him from a distance, too frightened to approach. But now he was here next to me, touching my face in a way that made me shiver in ecstasy. I traced his jawline. Sensations shot through my fingertips. It was the most wonderful feeling in the entire world. Nothing had ever felt anything like this. I traced his lips and ran my fingers across his eyelids and eyebrows.

"You're beautiful," I whispered to him. We sat in the corner touching each other's faces and arms and hands. "I was so down before," I said.

"I know." He kissed my fingertips.

"But you saved me." His act of generosity, his small gift, had helped me feel all this. He'd allowed me to fit in, to really fit in.

I loved everyone. I looked around the room at all these wonderful people, smiling so much that my face ached. After a while I went and sat with someone else, and we talked about our dreams and hopes. It was so easy. Each person in the room was a friend. I suddenly realized how well I knew them all. I cared about them all so much. I knew the secrets to the universe. I knew how humankind could live together in harmony. It was so obvious that people only wanted happiness. I'd unlocked the door to a hidden world. And it was heaven.

sophie

Dom's party seems like the place where everything began to unravel. But it wasn't. It really started long before that, before I even went out with him. It started with a lie and a big mistake. It's hard even to think about it, but maybe things wouldn't have become so awful if I'd never told that lie. It changed my friendship with Mia.

We were best friends. You hear girls say that all the time. "She's my best friend, blah, blah, blah," and then next week they've got a new one. But it wasn't like that for us. We'd been friends since kindergarten. All through school, if I needed a partner for something, that would be Mia. Everyone else knew it too, even the teachers. Sometimes it felt like we were treated as one person. And I didn't mind because Mia was the person I liked the best. Our friendship just worked without any effort. She'd make me laugh if I was down, or I'd solve her

17

problems if she was stuck. We talked about everything. There were no secrets.

Once, the two of us organized a camping trip during the summer holidays before the start of grade ten. We had a small tent, a stove, sleeping bags, a kerosene lamp, supplies in a cooler, a pack of cards, and some magazines. We loaded everything onto an ATV and drove it down the track to the edge of my family's property. There's five acres of bush with a clearing in the center where the house stands, surrounded by mowed lawn and tall scraggly oaks.

We pitched our tent, unrolled our sleeping bags, and set up our camping stove. Mia was cooking. She shook the pancake mixture in its plastic bottle and poured it into the pan. I sat back and watched—Mia knows exactly how to ham a situation up and put on a show. The pan kept slipping off the stove, it wasn't hot enough, or it was too hot and the pancakes started burning. She was trying to flip them in the air and ended up picking most of them up out of the dirt. It was dusk by the time she'd finished and we began chewing our way through the best parts. I told her how delicious they were, even with unidentifiable crunchy bits.

The gray of dusk deepened to darkness and we

turned the kerosene lamp on and huddled together in the tent. In the stillness outside I listened to the rustling of the bushes. Mia shifted nervously next to me, and when an owl started hooting she almost jumped out of her skin.

There was nothing to be scared of. I had a cell phone and Dad would've been down there in a shot.

"Do you ever get scared of stuff?" Mia said.

I nodded.

"I do too," she said. She was quiet for a minute, the shadows cast by the kerosene light elongating her features until she didn't look like Mia at all. "I'm scared of almost everything."

And she was. I'd known her most of her life. She hated change.

"I mean, it's like, what's happening next?" she said. "After school and stuff? What happens if you end up in some crap life?"

I thought she might have been thinking about her mom and dad.

"Yeah, but think of all the other stuff, like traveling the world," I said. I couldn't wait; I wasn't scared of change at all. All I was scared of were people's perceptions of me. I couldn't stand failure and I hated upsetting people or letting them down. I liked people to think I had it together, that I knew where I was going, that I would get what I wanted.

"But you know what else I'm scared of?" she said suddenly. "What if you and I weren't friends anymore? What if one day we didn't speak to each other?"

I sat in the strange shadows of the tent. As a possibility it seemed so remote. What could ever stop Mia and me from being friends?

"It'll never happen," I said easily. "We'll be friends forever."

I awoke to her high-pitched shriek. My face was pressed against the side of the tent and Mia was practically sitting on me.

"What is it?" I asked, wide awake and hoisting her off me in my scramble for the flashlight.

"Something touched my leg." Her knees were pulled up to her chin. "I think it's a snake."

I shone the flashlight around the tent. The bottom of the flap was unzipped just a bit, only enough to have let something in. I felt like laughing—it was probably a moth or something—but then I heard it, an ominous rattle. There was a quick flash as something slid underneath Mia's crumpled sleeping bag. I swung the flashlight back quickly, now fearful. Maybe it was a snake. I mentally assessed our escape route; we were closer to the opening than the snake. We could unzip the flap and scramble out before it realized it was trapped. I knew from my mother's warnings that you didn't want to trap a snake—it might turn on you.

"Unzip the doorway," I whispered to Mia, forgetting in my panic that snakes are deaf. Her hands were shaking as she reached across and slowly pulled the zip upward. I trained my flashlight back on the last sighting of the snake. There it was again, that noise. It was moving. It had to be a rattlesnake. I grabbed the cell with my other hand. "Go," I hissed. She didn't want to put her feet on the floor of the tent, but she didn't want to stay a second longer. In a very ungraceful movement she fell through the doorway, with me close behind.

"Shit, shit, shit," we chorused as we scrambled to our feet.

"What now?" she asked.

"Dunno," I said, zipping the flap up to keep the snake inside.

I phoned Dad and in minutes he was there.

"Is it still in there?" he asked.

I nodded. "I wasn't sure what to do. I trapped it."

"Go over there and sit on the ATV," he ordered.

Mia and I pulled our feet up onto the seat and watched him open the tent flap and gingerly begin moving the sleeping gear.

"Wow," he shouted, and Mia's nails dug into my arm. "Check out the size of this thing!"

"What is it?" I tried to sound normal, but terror has a funny way of making your voice high pitched.

"It's no rattlesnake," he said, turning his back on the snake still trapped in the tent. "It's not even a snake—it's a different species altogether."

"What?"

"Here's your snake, Mia," Dad said, reaching in to the tent and pulling out our tabby cat, Floyd. "*Felis catus*."

Floyd stared at us wide-eyed and shook his head indignantly, making his plastic bell rattle again. I laughed in relief.

But Mia was uncertain. "Are you sure that's all? It touched my leg and it felt scaly, not furry."

Dad smiled at her determination. "That's all there is, Mia. One domesticated house cat. Sorry, no snake!"

She attempted a smile, but she clearly wasn't one

hundred percent convinced. In her mind a snake, not a cat, had invaded the tent. And even in the face of irrefutable evidence, no one could convince her otherwise. She was so stubborn. But back then I accepted all that about her. She was my best friend.

So, why would I lie to her?

mia

I got home at seven the next morning. We'd danced and talked until dawn. I belonged to this group of beautiful people. It was the most amazing night of my life.

Lewis insisted on dropping me home. He gave Soph and Craig a lift too, dropping them off after me. Outside my house, he leaned across and gave me a light kiss on the lips. Beautiful, amazing Lewis Scott kissing me good-bye.

"I'll text you about tonight," he said as I shut the car door.

I nodded, too excited to speak, and watched his car take off, its rumbling engine rocking the silence of the early morning. I unlocked the front door quietly and stepped into the hallway, my shoes in my hand. I'd slipped them off the minute the E had kicked in, and my feet were filthy. The smell of rose potpourri hit me as I walked in. It's a smell that pervades our house. Mom is huge on smells.

I stopped in the hallway and listened. All was quiet as I crept to my room. Jordie's bedroom door was open. He was just a softly snoring mound under his duvet. I slid into the bathroom and locked the door behind me.

The image that stared back at me from the mirror was nothing like the vision I'd had of myself all night. I'd felt like a princess, golden and ethereal, but my reflection showed messy, matted hair and bloodshot eyes with dark rings under them. I looked away in disgust and turned the hot water on. Slowly the steam misted over my horrible image. I wanted to regain my inner vision, the one of beauty and confidence. I shampooed and scrubbed. I sat on the floor of the shower and shaved my legs. When I toweled myself dry I assessed my body in the mirror. My legs and bum were too big, and looking at them now I wondered what a guy like Lewis would think of me naked. I turned the light off and slipped into my bedroom.

I shut my eyes and tried to sleep, but it was impossible. I wasn't tired at all. I ran over every tiny detail, smiling when I remembered touching Lewis and sitting with him for hours. Even Craig and I had the most awesome conversation. I'd really misjudged him. He's a nice guy who made a big mistake–and was punished for it. I couldn't believe how judgmental I'd been toward him.

I lay back against the cool pillows. My bed smelled of newly laundered sheets. Every Friday Mom strips all the beds and remakes them with clean linen. I breathed in and rubbed my legs backward and forward against the smooth, crisp sheets. Ecstasy. I'd always thought I might try it one day. I'd heard kids at school talking about getting wasted on the weekends. They made it sound awesome. I pictured the roughly made tablets with their tiny butterflies. An amazing experience inside a tiny pill. How could something that made you feel like that be bad for you?

I'd heard the horror stories about people dying from ecstasy, and how it was a gateway to much worse drugs, but I also knew that it was mostly government propaganda and sensationalist stories to sell newspapers. Ecstasy was like anything else. If you did it safely, you'd be fine. The people who died were the ones who took stupid risks—or way too much. And people who went on to harder drugs were always going to do that anyway. I knew heaps of guys at school who'd smoked weed for years, and they'd never touched anything else. And last night everyone had been happy and in love. No one was aggressive or fighting. Last night people were glorious.

I couldn't stay in bed any longer. I felt so restless. Not in a bad way, but running over every detail, trying to recapture the tranquility and peace. I dressed and went into the kitchen. Last year Mom spent a fortune on a new kitchen, so now it looked like something out of *House Beautiful*. She is meticulous about keeping it perfect. Everything has to be in its place.

I poured myself some orange juice. The fridge door was

still open when Mom walked in. She kicked at it lightly with her foot and used the sleeve of her dressing gown to rub away my fingerprints as she flicked the kettle on.

"How was last night?" she asked, getting out her favorite cup, which has *thirty* written on it even though she's really thirty-eight.

"Good," I said, drinking my juice and flicking through yesterday's paper.

"When did you get in?"

"This morning. Soph had modeling, so I walked home."

It was partly true. Soph did have modeling. But I was deliberately making Mom think I'd stayed the night at Sophie's when in fact we'd never left the party.

Last night was the first time since Dad had left that Mom let me go out without someone's parent taking me or picking me up. She's been totally overprotective. It's like she has to prove that she's this supermom. But Damon, her boyfriend, has been at her about lightening up. When I asked if I could go to Dominic's party it was Damon who supported me.

"Rae, she's fifteen," he'd said when Mom frowned at my suggestion that Sophie and I could find our own way home. "Think about what you were doing when you were that age."

That stopped her. My grandma had been really strict with Mom when she was my age. Mom had told me how all she'd ever wanted was a bit of trust and freedom.

"You take your phone and call me when you get there," she said finally.

I was so happy I hugged both of them. "Thanks," I said, "you're awesome."

So I didn't want her to think I'd taken advantage of her trust. She'd freak if she thought I'd been out all night. And go completely psycho if she knew about the E. The best thing to do was let her believe I'd been at Soph's.

"You're supposed to be at your dad's at eleven," Mom said, getting the milk out of the fridge.

"Do I have to go?" Last night Lewis had asked if I wanted to go to a dance party. I could only imagine what it would be like, feeling that way in a room with hundreds of people soaking up the rhythm of the universe. And to go with Lewis Scott!

"It's your dad's weekend."

"I know, but I've got stuff to do. I'm meeting with Soph tonight, and anyway, I don't want to be around Kylie."

"I thought you liked her." Mom looked at me over the top of her cup.

"She's getting too big for herself now. Thinks she can talk to me like she's my friend, or my mother."

Mom winced. The subject of Kylie is still painful for her. Dad and Kylie had been business partners, and he'd left home a month before my twelfth birthday to be with her. Even though Mom's got a new boyfriend and has moved on from the train wreck of her marriage, Kylie still touches a nerve.

"You'll have to call him," she said finally. "I don't want him thinking I've put you up to this. You'll have to tell him that you've got your own life now."

Fine with me. Dad was a pushover anyway.

I didn't know what to do with myself. I was in limbo, waiting for Lewis to text me but worried he might not. I studied myself in the mirror. There was a monumental pimple lurking beneath the surface of my chin. I didn't want it erupting tonight. But it wasn't ready to squeeze, and anyway that could be deadly–turning it into a mountain worthy of its own zip code. I stopped myself from touching it and plucked a few stray hairs out of my eyebrows. Then I gave myself a pedicure. My poor heel was so sore. I was sticking on a bandage when my cell vibrated. A message from Lewis!

party on. pick u up @ mall @ 8

Immediately I texted Sophie. My stomach was fluttering as I assessed my wardrobe. I had to wear something ultra cool. He had to think I was hot. The shoes posed the biggest problem–what could I wear without turning into a cripple? My phone buzzed again.

cant mom freakd bout 2 much partyn

No way! I needed Soph there. I wasn't ready to do it on my own. Her parents are super strict. In fact, her mom's a mega control freak, picking on Sophie for just about everything. Nothing is ever good enough for Mrs. Spencer. First she thinks Soph spends too much time at my house—but then she says I'm a good influence because I'm sensible and don't go stupid over every guy I see. She says this in front of Soph. Can you imagine how bad that makes Soph feel? We both hate her.

say ur @ my place my mom out tonite I'll b @ yours

Her message came back.

ok meet at mall

I was smiling happily. It was going to be another great night.

I called Dad, but Kylie answered.

"Can I speak to Dad?" I asked.

"Sure, sure," she said and put the phone down. She knew I was still mad after the argument we'd had last time I was there.

I'd always got along pretty well with Kylie. And Mom had always tried not to slag her in front of us. So I guess I'd never really thought about how hard it was for Mom to let us stay with her and Dad. Anyway, the visit before, Kylie had taken me out and bought me a bra. It was pink, with underwire and rhinestones. I loved it. When I got home I showed it to Mom.

"That's nice," she said, smiling. But her face was tight and her eyes weren't smiling. Her reaction really bothered me. I sat in my room trying to figure out why she was so hurt when I suddenly understood. She didn't want Kylie buying me things that a mother should buy. She didn't want Kylie taking me to expensive lingerie stores and having me professionally fitted instead of getting one off the rack at Target. From where Mom was standing, Kylie had taken her husband and now she was trying to take her children. I felt so ashamed for betraying my mom like that and an overwhelming rush of hatred for Kylie.

So when I saw Kylie next I dropped the bra in its plastic bag in her lap.

"What's all this?" she asked nervously. She'd known from the minute I'd arrived that something was going on. I could barely look at her. I was so angry with myself. I felt like I'd knifed my own mother in the back.

"Your bra," I said. "I don't want it."

"Oh," Kylie said, opening the bag and looking at it. "I thought you did. I thought it fitted you really well. You said it was so much nicer than the ones your–"

I cut her off. "Shut up. Don't you dare talk about my mother."

Her face went bright red and she looked at me, shocked. "I just thought, after what you said–"

I jumped up and pointed my finger at her. "Don't," I said. "I told you to shut up."

And then I ran to the bedroom Jordie and I shared

when we stayed over. I didn't want to hear the mean things she was going to say about my mom, about her awful taste in clothes, and how she tried to dress me like a little girl. I didn't want to hear her repeat the things that I'd told her when we'd laughed, like friends, about my mother.

Now Dad came on the phone.

"Hi, honey," he said. "Tell your mom to bring you over in an hour or so. I'm just running to the store. Chocolate chip or caramel?"

Whenever I hear my dad's voice like that it makes me aware of how much I miss him. I knew he was going to be disappointed, but he was the one who'd left so he could "have a life"—it was only fair I should have one too.

"I can't come this weekend, Dad," I said. "I've got a party to go to."

He was silent. Don't be pissed off with me, I thought. This is your fault anyway. "It's a huge one, I can't miss it," I said to break the silence.

"But it's our weekend." He sounded hurt.

"I know, sorry. But, Dad, this is like the event of the year. You wouldn't want your daughter to be the biggest loser of the century, would you?"

"As if you could," he said. "When will I see you?"

"I'll come next weekend. I'm sure Mom won't mind," I said quickly. "I'll get her to call you."

When Mom got home after dropping Jordie off, I heard her rattling around in the kitchen. She was slamming cupboard doors and ferociously wiping the countertops.

"What's up?" I asked her as I came out of the bathroom with my hair in a towel.

"Your damn father wasn't even there," she muttered, grabbing the phone. "He knows I don't like leaving Jordie on his own with her."

For the first time Mom was expressing how she felt about Kylie. I guess she knew I was jumping camps and that she finally had an ally.

"Maybe you should phone him later," I suggested gently. In this mood Mom was walking straight into a massive fight. "Jordie's nearly eight now, Mom, not the baby he used to be."

"I can handle your father," she said, waving me away. And I didn't know if that was meant to be ironic.

I didn't have to eavesdrop to hear her conversation. I think the neighbors three doors down heard it too. She berated him for not being there and then moved on to me. "No, Matt, you can't force her. She's nearly sixteen. She's entitled to her own social life."

There was a pause, for a second. "Well, whose fault is

that? If you'd cared about spending time with her four years ago, you wouldn't have left her for that slut."

She screamed the last word and slammed the phone down against the kitchen bench. It's the fourth handset we've had in as many years. I never heard Mom and Dad fight so much when they were together. It seems like a lifetime ago when we were this happy family, the four of us, doing family stuff together. And then it ended. In one afternoon Dad announced he was in love with another woman and walked out the door.

Mom was sitting in front of the smashed phone, staring off into space. It's a look she's fine-tuned over the last few years. She gave me her I'm-exhausted-but-I-have-to-put-on-a-good-front-for-my-kids smile.

"I'm thinking I might ring Damon and cancel tonight. Why don't we stay home and have a girls' night in. Pizza and movies, hey?" she suggested, reaching for my hand.

Ordinarily, I would have fallen over myself to hang out with her. Most weekends when we weren't at Dad's I stayed home looking after Jordie while she went out with Damon. I was glad she'd got a life, but I ended up with lonely nights of chick flicks and chat rooms. Sometimes Soph would come over, but more and more lately she'd be off to a party. I'd have given anything for Mom to stay home with me then, but now it was my turn to go out and have fun.

"Sorry, Mom, I've got to do this work with Sophie

tonight," I lied, looking her in the eye. She dropped her gaze immediately, and I knew it was because she was grateful she didn't have to give up her evening with Damon.

"Are you staying the night, or do you want me to pick you up?" she asked. "We'll probably be back about midnight."

"Nah, I'll stay. If we finish early we're going to stay up and watch some movies." I felt bad lying to her, but I was confident she wouldn't check it out with Sophie's mom. I've never given Mom any reason to doubt me, ever. I think I'd lied more in one day than I had in my whole life.

After Mom left I surveyed my wardrobe again. I wished I had another new outfit. I need all the help I can get. I'm not a standout in the crowd–pretty average-looking in fact, with shoulder-length brown hair that I wish was blonde like Sophie's. I want layers and highlights, but Mom won't let me. "Why ruin its beautiful color with chemicals?" she says, even though it's a mousy brown.

Luckily I have pretty good skin, even if the freckles on my nose seem to get darker every year. And I'm in pretty good shape, though the tops of my thighs are definitely jiggly and my bum is too big. I wish I had Sophie's boobs. Mine are more like small pimples. Some days I think they'll never grow.

The whole situation was surreal. And scary. Lewis is in grade twelve and one of the most popular guys in school. According to Sophie, he is the life of every party. I can't believe he noticed me. Last night was like a dream, talking together for hours, and now he's texting me like I'm his girlfriend. If only *I* could have someone like *him*. I had to look hot–now that I had his attention I had to keep it.

sophie

Have you ever done something so stupid, the memory of it makes you physically cringe? You wipe your hand across your eyes wishing you could erase the image, but the memory creeps up on you when you're doing something else, and you're experiencing it all over again, as potent as ever?

It was at Cherie's birthday party at a Chinese restaurant, early in grade ten. Mom dropped Mia and me off, assuming that Cherie's parents would be there. They weren't. It was banquet style, with as much wine and beer as we wanted, the waiters all ignoring the fact we were so obviously underage. You can imagine what happened.

Szechuan noodles and fried rice flew through the air, landed on other diners, and on the walls. One girl was vomiting in a potted plant. The restaurant people got really mad, they screamed at us and so we all took off in a drunken hurry. We ended up in a park cleaning ourselves up in some smelly public toilets. I was feeling pretty sick; every time I shut my eyes I felt like I was whooshing down a tunnel, really fast. So I sat on the toilet seat and pushed my hands against the walls and tried to slow my head down. I could hear the others outside laughing.

I'd been sitting in there a while when the cubicle door opened and I felt a hand on my head. I looked up to see Thomas Westcroft standing there.

He crouched down and asked me if I was all right. "I was worried about you," he said.

The next thing I knew we were making out in the cubicle. And here is the worst part. I've heard girls say, "I don't remember what happened, I was so out of it," and I've thought, Bullshit. No one's ever so out of it they don't know what's happening. Well, I do remember parts of it. But not all of it, or how I went from one thing to the next. But I wasn't forced into it by Thomas.

I'd never done anything more than kiss a guy. In grade eight I got a bit heavy with a boy called Marcus, but it was winter and I had on a couple of layers of thick clothes. With Thomas it was flesh on flesh. We didn't go all the way, but I think I would've if he'd pushed me to. That's how drunk I was. I did what I'd heard guys really like, and what most girls at my school think isn't really sex. I gave him a blow job.

I can still smell the stench of that toilet. The whole thing was horrible. Once I'd started, I wanted it over quickly. It wasn't what I expected. None of the magazines tell you how hard it is to breathe, how it makes you choke and gag, or how long it takes. My jaw cramped and I wanted to vomit. It's the best-kept secret, how revolting it is for us girls.

When it was over I didn't want to look at him. I couldn't believe what I'd done. I felt so degraded, so completely humiliated. But he was busy zipping his pants up and tucking his shirt in. He seemed so pleased with himself—and suddenly I felt completely sober. "Well, let's go back then," he said.

I couldn't look at him. I didn't want people to see us leaving the toilet together. I didn't want them all guessing what had just happened. Which is funny now, because what girls want to keep private, guys have this need to share. But I didn't know that then. Thomas left, and as I washed my face, I heard a cheer from the park. I think my blood actually froze for a second. I stared at myself in the mirror through the graffiti, under the flickering blue lights they use to stop junkies from finding their veins, and saw Mia appear behind me.

She put her arm around me. "You okay?"

And I knew she knew because she looked at me with such pity. They all knew. Thomas had gone straight out there and told everyone what I'd done. I nodded, but I started crying anyway.

So, that was my mistake. I'd always been in control of everything I did. And I hated feeling like I'd lost that control. I'd always thought girls who'd done it must be sophisticated, mature, knowledgeable. But that's not how I felt. I felt used and dirty, stupid and slutty. And everyone at school knew. Thomas was the big stud and I was that chick who got drunk and gave head. Except for Mia, it felt like everyone suddenly saw me differently. They felt sorry for me, like I was a victim. Weak and pathetic. That was almost the worst thing of all.

And I guess that's what started the lie.

mia

Sophie was sitting on the low brick wall outside the mall. She looked fantastic. She is one of the most beautiful people I've ever met. She has a model's face, with perfect skin and teeth. With her face and personality she doesn't have to try hard to get attention. When people meet her, they just stare; her gigantic blue eyes seem to enchant them. Though guys don't often make eye contact with her—they usually can't take their eyes off her breasts.

"Boys like boobs more than we understand," she says. And she'd know. She has flirting down to an exact science; she can get any guy she wants. Though maybe that's also because guys know she'll give them what they want.

Soph's been with heaps of guys, starting last year when, absolutely hammered, she gave Thomas Westcroft a blow job. It was around the school in a flash. I was secretly horrified that she'd done it—the thought of putting that in my mouth–gross!–makes me shudder. But together we decided that because she was drunk it hadn't been her fault–you can't be held responsible if you're so out of it you don't know what you're doing. Even so, she cried about it for two weeks solid. I felt terrible for her. But then she turned it all around and went from the school's object of pity to the most desirable girl in our grade. Guys virtually lined up to go out with her. Soph had her pick of anyone she wanted. She was in one relationship after another. She told me everything, so one day she admitted to me how she'd finally gone all the way. In that instant things between us changed. We'd always been equal, done everything together– kindergarten, ballet, rollerblading–now, suddenly, she was way ahead of me. I'd always imagined we'd be the same age when we finally did it, but the closest I'd got was when Peter Brand tried to feel me up in grade eight. He stuck his hand up my skirt, but I was so embarrassed I made him stop. Listening to Sophie talk about it made her seem so much older than me. She went from being my best friend to my older sister. It wasn't so bad. It was just different.

For Sophie, having sex is just a normal part of relationships. I get the impression that once you crack the seal it's hard to go back to hand-holding. I was wondering if Craig might be the new guy. I don't know where they went after Lewis dropped them off, but I knew she'd tell me all the gossip.

"So," she said when I sat down, "is Lewis picking us up?"

"Yep." It was hard not to be too excited. "Can you believe it?"

"Of course," she said. "Look at you—he's not blind."

But I couldn't think about him, not when he might turn up at any second. "So what happened with you and Craig?" I said to change the subject.

"He's nice," she said.

"Did you?" I asked.

"No." She shook her head. "It was way too intense. I don't think I could've handled it."

"It was wild," I said, nodding in agreement. "The E was amazing."

"Yeah," she said, "it was better than I thought it would be."

"It was so …" But I couldn't describe the way it made me feel.

Sophie was nodding her head anyway, she completely understood. "Yeah, what a night."

"Hey, what was up with Dominic? I saw you two talking."

Soph shrugged. "Nothing, really. It was just about nothing."

I kept looking for Lewis's car; I felt nervous as anything.

"Are you going to do it again tonight?" Soph asked.

"I think so. If he offers I will," I said. The ecstasy had made me feel so confident. I didn't know if he'd like me if I was just me.

We watched him pull into the car park in his metallic blue car. His parents are mega rich and have this massive house down by the beach. I've never been there, but I know which one it is. All the kids at the school do.

He had the music up loud. "Hi," he said, leaning out the window, "you girls want a lift?"

The inside of his car was immaculate. I got into the front and sank into the seat, hoping he couldn't hear my heart thumping madly.

"This is Glenn." He jerked his thumb toward a guy sprawled across the back seat. Where Lewis was clean and ironed, Glenn looked like he'd just crawled out of bed. He was crumpled and messy, with dirty black stubble on his face. Sophie squeezed in next to him.

"Hi," she said breathlessly. "I'm Sophie, and that's Mia."

sophie

I keep procrastinating. I know. I'm an expert at it. I don't want to be, but I do love that word, *procrastinating*. Once, our English teacher was getting really fed up with this guy in our class, Brandon Bent. She was standing at the front trying to get us to draw up charts and Brandon was fiddling with his iPod, his bag, his books, anything. He hadn't read the novel. Anyway, his hands were rummaging around in his bag, which was on his lap, when she finally lost it and shouted at him: "Brandon, stop procrastinating!"

He stopped and looked at her, horrified.

"I'm reporting you, miss," he said, his cheeks bright red.

"What for?" She was laughing by then. She's got a pretty good sense of humor, Miss Lawler.

"What you just said."

And I figure that's why she said it—because she knew what he'd think. "What was that?"

"For saying I'm wanking," he said.

She just laughed again and dropped the dictionary on his desk. "Look it up, Brandon, then write the definition on the board."

> *Procrastinating: deferring action, lagging, postponing work (especially out of laziness or habitual carelessness).*

So I keep procrastinating. But it's not laziness. There's more I need to explain first.

For two hellish weeks after the Westcroft job I could hardly cope. I felt like I'd ruined everything. I even thought about telling my mom—for one insane nanosecond. God, the thought of *that* makes me feel ill even now. When I think about all the times I've heard my mom talk about me to her friends—about how I know myself and would never be swayed by peer pressure, about how strong and smart I am—if she knew, she'd never look at me in the same way again, and that's more than I could handle.

As always, Mia was my lifeline. She told me to go easy on myself. She helped me deflect comments, especially from Thomas and his scumbag friends. She even managed to make me laugh about it.

Once, Thomas was standing near us at assembly and whispered, loud enough for people nearby to hear: "Wanna give it another blow, Soph?"

And Mia said, even more loudly: "Sorry, Thomas, I've told Sophie not to put small things in her mouth that she might choke on."

And of course everyone—except Thomas—laughed. Even me.

So here is my secret. Not only am I a procrastinator, I'm a virgin too. A big fat virgin.

If you'd asked Mia, she would have told you I'd done it with lots of guys. Not that she would've told you anything. She'd have told you to mind your own business. But under a lie detector test, say, that's what she would've said. Because that's what I told her. Of course, you're wondering why, after being publicly humiliated and having my dignity dragged through the mud, would I make up such a thing?

This is how it happened.

A couple of weeks after my little tryst with Thomas,

my history class was doing research in the library and I was hiding behind the magazine rack reading *Teen Vogue.* I'd already finished the assignment at home. In an ironic twist, my marks had improved because I'd imposed a ban on all socializing—it was possible I might never go out in public again. I was certainly never drinking again. So, study pressure was off, my parents were pleased, and my teachers were impressed. In fact, if only I could've just erased fifteen sordid minutes from my past, my life would have been perfect. But I couldn't, so hiding from the staring faces and whispered comments was my new plan.

"Whatchya doing?"

I looked up to see Ryan Windsor leaning against the bookcase watching me.

A quick profile on Ryan Windsor:

Tall and well built.

Blond-tipped hair.

Pale green eyes and golden tan.

White teeth, slightly crooked, but no need for major dental work.

A year older.

And, to put it as nicely as possible, an IQ of about room temperature.

"Reading," I said.

I guess I was expecting some sort of jibe, a prod, a dirty comment, but instead he said, "Any good?"

I frowned and glanced up. He looked a bit pink-faced, and his foot scuffed the carpet. He was nervous. Then I understood why Ryan had come over. And in a second a light rush of electricity surged through my body, a tingling of power.

"Not really." I dropped the magazine on the floor and wriggled backward in my beanbag. The polystyrene rustled loudly in the library's stillness. "What about you? What are you doing?" And it wasn't really me, it was this powerful other persona that flicked my hair back and looked up at him through my lashes. I know it sounds corny, but you should've seen it work.

He took a step closer.

"I was wondering if ..." He didn't know what to say. He was embarrassed.

I laughed a soft, encouraging laugh. "Yes?"

He crouched down next to me. "I was wondering ... if you'd like to go out with me." His cheeks grew redder. "Friday night? To the movies? Maybe, if you're not busy."

I swear to you, I had no control over the situation. I felt like I was possessed by some kind of goddess because

I knew exactly, instinctively, what to do. I also knew that if anything was going to save me from a lifetime of self-imposed seclusion it was this. With my self-esteem around my ankles, it felt like a step in the right direction.

"Friday," I said, like I was flicking the pages of a mental diary. "Yeah, okay. That'd be cool."

"Cool," he echoed. "Yeah, okay. Shall I meet you at the bus stop in front of the mall?"

"Yeah." I nodded and picked up my magazine, dismissing him. "I'll see you then. Say six."

After he left I pulled myself together. What was I doing? Did he think taking me out was going to get him some action? I had to tread carefully, poised as I was with one foot in slut camp.

And funnily enough, it went well.

Ryan, for all his missing IQ points, was actually really nice. He didn't try anything more than putting an arm around me and a fumbled kiss at the end of the night. And when I kissed him I felt it again. He was intimidated by me! It was so weird. I was at the lowest point in my life and a popular, good-looking guy was intimidated by me.

I didn't go out with him again. I didn't have to. Because by Monday I was asked out by Dion. And a pattern emerged, with a new guy every Friday night.

And I didn't have to do anything more than kiss them. All I had to do was move on to the next carefully chosen guy. I wasn't with anyone long enough for them to expect me to do anything I didn't want to do.

As the weeks passed and my popularity grew I began to see myself in a better light. I'd made a mistake that I had no intention of repeating, at least not until I wanted to do it with someone I really cared about. Sober. And here's something else—while guys will brag about what they *have* done, most keep their mouths shut about what they *haven't*. And, unlike Thomas, these guys were nice, so not one of them was prepared to talk about how far they got with Sophie Spencer anyway. Somehow I'd found myself on very desirable ground. It was all to do with which boy you hooked up with. Now I had all the appearances of being cool and popular and none of the hangups of a bad reputation.

Things changed for me and Mia. Now we got invited to join groups of older guys. And it seemed really cool. Other girls' looks of pity were replaced with looks of envy. And Mia started to look up to me, like I knew so much more than she did. I felt like a worldly older sister. She thought I was brave. And experienced. Mia really believed me.

Then I went out with Tony. He was a totally hot guy in grade eleven—great-looking, funny, and smart—and when he asked me out I was so excited. For the first time I broke my rule and I went out with Tony again and again.

I met his mom and dad and his sister, Isabella, and then before I knew it we were celebrating our one-month anniversary. But by now Tony was getting impatient with just kissing.

"Soph," he'd whisper in my ear while he pressed himself against me, hard. "Soph." He was practically begging, and though I really liked him, the thought of going further terrified me. It was like I was in that filthy toilet stall again. I'd wriggle out of the clinch, ignore his plea, but every time we went out, he just put more pressure on me.

The only way to stop it was to break up. It nearly killed me. But I just couldn't go any further. So I dumped him.

Mia and I were on our bench where we always used to sit when it was just us. I was pretty upset, telling her that Tony and I'd split. I cried. Mia didn't understand why I was so distraught when I was the one who'd dumped him.

"So why, then?" she asked, squeezing my hand. I wanted to tell her how I felt pressured to have sex, but I didn't want her thinking badly of Tony. And as I tried to figure out how to tell her that I was still freaked by what had happened with Thomas Westcroft, she said, "I guess I don't understand what it's like to split up with someone you've done it with."

I nearly choked. Mia was looking at the ground and her cheeks were pink. How could she think that of me?

And then, without looking up, really softly, she asked, "What was it like, Soph? Was it how you thought it would be?"

She handed it to me. That feeling of power you get when you know something other people don't. That feeling of importance. And I took it. I liked having her look up to me. I'd felt so low I never thought anyone would respect me again. And here it was—though in retrospect it isn't something I want to be admired for. But I took it. Everything on offer I took. And as the words came out of my mouth it was that other me talking, the self-confident and experienced me. I opened my mouth and out came this new self.

And that was my big stupid lie. Almost immediately I wanted to drop it, but I just couldn't. How could I admit to having lied? It would've made me seem like the biggest loser ever. So I became the lie and the lie became me. I even—and this is so pathetic to admit—researched stuff on the Internet so that what I told her would be credible. I know I acted badly. But this is the nature of liars. The world we live in is like quicksand—once you've put a toe in, you've had it. And then I really turned into that girl. I forgot what I used to be like—a bit shy and a lot insecure—and I became the confident person my mom always thought I was. A self-assured girl that guys really liked. And not one of them got anything more than a kiss out of me. Except Dominic. I fell in love with Dominic Cimino.

mia

I kept sneaking looks at Lewis as we drove through the streets. He had the stereo up loud, some techno music that I didn't know, and his fingers were drumming the rhythm on the gearshift. I tried to loosen up and find the beat, but I was totally nervous. Sophie and Glenn were talking to each other. What did she think of to say? I desperately wanted to engage Lewis in conversation, but there was nothing. Sweet FA. Yet Soph could meet someone and in seconds have them telling her his life story.

We drove into an industrial area, and finally Lewis pulled into a driveway that led to a massive warehouse. As we got near, the beat of the music spilled out and seemed to vibrate through the walls of the car. Lewis pulled up to the curb and I looked out the window at people darting through the darkness wearing green-and-yellow neon bracelets and necklaces. Little slivers of light moving through thin air.

Lewis turned to the two in the back. "Before we go in ..." he said, putting his hand out to Glenn.

Glenn shuffled around and pulled a plastic ziplock bag out of his back pocket. He flicked it to Lewis. Inside it were at least twenty yellow pills.

Seeing the pills made me feel both nervous and relieved. The E would surely help me relax. I didn't want to blow my chance with Lewis. "Are they the same as last night?" I asked as he picked one out and handed it to me.

"Yep," he said, and threw two in his mouth, swigged from a bottle of Evian, and handed the bottle to me.

I swallowed one pill and cold water flooded the area behind my rib cage.

"Soph?" he asked, offering her the bag. She looked at me and almost frowned, then popped one while Glenn popped two. I smiled at her. We were okay. She smiled back. Lewis opened my door and helped me out of the car.

"Ever been to one of these before?" he shouted in my ear as we approached the entrance. The music was thumping out the door.

I shook my head. Through the doorway I saw flashing lights and hundreds and hundreds of pulsating bodies. "Don't leave me," I shouted back, and he tightened his grip on my hand.

It was a galaxy of people, and I loved them all. I absorbed the music through my skin. As I danced, the music flooded into every atom of my body until I was the music. I was an electronic machine. It was wild and fast and hot. Everything felt so good. I felt a little tipsy, but I was in complete control. I knew I could talk to anyone without looking like an idiot or sounding wasted. I knew I could dance all night long without looking like a sloppy drunk. The feeling of control was powerful.

I touched Lewis. His eyes were shut, his hair was wet, and the beat was surging through his body. He opened his eyes and smiled at me. Then he put his arms around me and pulled me close. The next minute we were kissing so intensely I felt his tongue against every tooth. I wanted to kiss him harder, get inside of him. His hands were under my top and my skin was literally vibrating.

Then he grabbed hold of my hand and led me through the pulsating bodies. I looked for Sophie, but I couldn't see her. But it didn't matter I would've gone anywhere with Lewis. I bumped into people and trod on toes as I followed him out of the building, but everybody whose eyes I met sent me their good vibes. No one was aggressive. Everyone smiled and touched me. And every time I was touched it was like another connection. A new bond. I was touched by them all. They were all beautiful and I loved them.

Outside I realized how hot I was. The air was cool and my cheeks were on fire.

"I'm hot," I said, pulling at his hand to stop him.

He looked back at me. "Christ, Mia, you're bright red. I can't believe I forgot the water."

We walked to his car and I leaned against the door as he pulled out a small cooler. It was filled with half a dozen bottles of water. I looked at them longingly as he unscrewed one and handed it to me. It was the most pure thing I've ever tasted. Clear and clean and utterly refreshing. I chugged it down and was reaching for another when Lewis grabbed my hand.

"Go easy, Mia. Drinking too much water can be as bad as dehydration."

"What?" How could pure water be bad for you?

"A girl died. She drank heaps of water, way too much, and it diluted her blood. Her brain was swollen."

"Yeah, yeah." I gulped down more water. "Everyone's so paranoid."

When I listened to Sophie talk about sex, the idea of actually doing it filled me with dread. I was terrified it would hurt. Or worse, that the whole thing would be embarrassing because I wouldn't know what to do. But I don't think I can put into words what it was like with Lewis. Even though it was in the back of his car, everything was perfect, especially the way he looked at me and touched me. I wanted him so much that I didn't feel any shame or embarrassment. I'd never felt so close to anyone before, so totally connected. I felt his heart hammering through my chest.

It felt like hours had passed when I opened my eyes again. Lewis was sitting back, eyes shut. In the half-light he looked so relaxed, so happy, and it filled me with pride. I was responsible for that. I'd just had sex with Lewis Scott! I'd finally done it, and with the biggest sex god ever. I couldn't wait to tell Sophie.

I looked out the window. There was no one around, so I jumped out of the car to put my pants back on. I stood half behind a tree and the car door. As I turned my clothes the right way round I felt something wet running down the inside of my leg. Another time I might've freaked out. Yuck! They didn't talk about that in sex ed!

In the backseat, Lewis was moving around, getting dressed as well. "Mia," he said softly.

I looked at him through the gap between the front seats. He was so beautiful. "Yeah?"

"Was that your first time?" he asked.

I nodded my head. "It's been a weekend of first times."

We sat on the hood of his car looking at the stars and drinking water. Lewis thought Glenn and Soph would come to the car when they realized we'd left the building, so we lay against the windshield, arms touching, and talked. There was so much to say. He told me about his parents, who own their own business. His parents always travel and are often away for months at a time. Lewis said I'd have to come to his place and swim in the pool—which is heated year-round. I couldn't believe all the stuff we talked about. It was a fantasy come true. Invisible Mia and Dream God Lewis.

After a long while Soph and Glenn still hadn't turned up, and Lewis suggested we go down to the beach.

"Shouldn't we go back inside and get them?" I asked, sliding off the hood.

"There's thousands of people in there, Mia; we'll never find them." He grabbed my hand and pulled me close. "Glenn'll look after her. Don't worry, Sophie's a big girl. Besides, I kind of like having you all to myself."

I grinned. Things just kept getting better. He was right. Sophie could look after herself. As we drove away, Lewis reached over and held my hand. I relaxed back in the seat, marveling that this was really me.

When we got to the beach Lewis rummaged around under the passenger seat and pulled out a yellow ceramic bong with a marijuana leaf painted on the side. Most guys I know use a plastic bottle with a metal stem stuck in the side.

"We should have a cone," he said. "It'll stop the rolling and bring you back down. Help you sleep."

I nodded my head. I didn't think I'd survive another sleepless night.

"Had one before?" he said as he offered me the bong.

"Nah. I've only smoked joints." It was sort of true. I'd once had a puff, but it had burnt my throat and made me nauseous.

"I'll help. When I light it you have to suck, really hard. Then when I say now, you inhale."

"Okay." I put my mouth over the top of the bong. Lewis lit the weed and held his finger over the hole.

"Ready ... inhale now," he said, taking his finger off the hole.

I choked so hard my throat caught fire. I coughed and

spluttered and tears ran down my face. I couldn't breathe. Every time I thought I'd caught my breath I'd splutter and choke some more.

Lewis laughed and said it happened to everyone, even him sometimes. He opened another bottle of water and handed it to me. I watched him have a cone, quickly and painlessly. Then he opened the car door and emptied the bong, rinsed it out with bottled water, and stuck it back under the seat.

"Stops it from stinking up the car," he said. "You don't want to spill old bong water. You never get rid of the smell."

I smiled. Lewis knew so much about everything. He came around and opened my door. Despite all the coughing and choking, I was really stoned. My eyes were heavy. My body was heavy. I held his hand and we trudged down to the beach. It was dark and things scurried through the bushes in the dunes. Any other time I would have been frightened of snakes, or perverts, but not tonight. Not with Lewis Scott. He made me feel completely safe. With Lewis I knew nothing bad could ever happen to me.

We lay down on the sand. Lewis had brought a blanket from the car. He thought of everything. He put his arm underneath my neck and pulled me close. I still couldn't believe it. The grin that had been stretched across my face was making my muscles ache. I don't know how long I lay there listening to his heart beat and the steady crashing of the waves, thinking how everything was so perfect.

Lewis's breathing was getting slower and I felt myself nodding off. Suddenly he said, "I've got the munchies. Shall we get some McDonald's?"

I didn't want to move. I wanted to stay on the beach with him forever. But my mouth was dry and I was hungry, so I nodded my head and slowly sat up. "Yeah, I'd kill for a chocolate shake."

At the drive-thru Lewis ordered enough food for about twenty people. I was going through the loose change in my purse when he said, "Hey, I'll get it. I pay when I take a girl out."

Inwardly I was ecstatic; we were really going out then!

When he dropped me home I leaned across and kissed him. It was long, deep, and passionate, and I surprised myself with how self-assured I felt. "See you later," I said, hoping it didn't sound like a question.

"Definitely," he said, putting the car into reverse. "I'll call you."

I stood on the doorstep and watched him drive off. I saw his hand wave at me through the open window as he turned the corner, out of sight.

When I woke in the morning I lay back and shut my eyes again, running through everything we'd done. I'd had sex. With Lewis Scott! I felt so different. Now I knew what Sophie was talking about. It had been perfect. A decision that I would never regret. I hugged myself, wishing it was his arms around me.

My body ached and my face was sore—I guess from smiling so much. I don't remember ever laughing more. A new world had opened up for me, a place where I was confident and beautiful and a hot guy like Lewis wanted to be with me. That morning I figured life couldn't get any better.

sophie

I went out with Dominic for three months, four days, and six hours. There was not one single thing I didn't like about him. Talk about nice, kind, and totally gorgeous. Talk about funny, smart, compassionate, and sensitive, and you'd be talking about him. Dom would do anything for you, even go clothes shopping. But he wasn't a wimp. He had a load of friends, he surfed, and he was a football player too. The ultimate, most perfect boyfriend.

The only downside was that I was in a constant state of tension about him. We'd go so far, and then I'd have to remind myself that I did not want to go all the way. I'd made the decision that I really wanted to wait until I'd finished high school. That was the person I saw myself as—someone able to hold it all together and keep control. So there was my brain fiercely guarding my virginity, while my body kept screaming at me that *it* was ready. Dominic was the one. I knew that if I was going to do anything, it would be with him.

So one day I let his skin touch my skin. It felt so good. But then I panicked. We were going too far, we had to stop, and I shoved him away from me.

"Soph, what is it?" He grabbed hold of my shoulders. I think he thought I'd gone mad. I was crying and shaking and pushing him away. I couldn't look at him.

He tried to turn my face up toward him. "I didn't mean to upset you. God, Soph, I'm so sorry. I thought you wanted to."

And suddenly, I completely freaked. Something tripped in my head and I totally lost it. It was like Dominic was Thomas Westcroft, and I said and did all the things I wished I'd done the year before.

"Leave me alone," I screamed at him. "Don't you dare touch me. Let me go."

And I ran, shoes in hand, out of his house, past his startled mother and into the street.

He called me. He came over and tried to talk to me. But I felt utterly humiliated by my performance. How could I possibly explain? I couldn't. It seemed like everything had got so tangled up—because I'd created this stupid fictional life that I was now trapped in. I could almost see the humor in it. I desperately wanted to tell Mia everything, but I couldn't because my friendship with her was now based on the same fiction, and it was nobody's fault but mine. I had no idea what to do. I felt so stupid.

mia

It was about two o'clock in the afternoon before I got out of bed. I guess all that missed sleep finally caught up with me. I heard Mom come into my room a couple of times to get me up, but I pretended I was still sleeping and drifted off again. When I finally did get up I sat yawning on the edge of the bed, watching Mom through the window, weeding. The sight of her working made me want to curl up under the duvet and shut my eyes again. But I had to get up. I had an English assignment due the next day.

I stood in the bathroom and looked at myself in the mirror. I didn't look noticeably different. No one would know, unless I told them, that I wasn't a virgin anymore.

I sat at my desk and tried to write about internal conflict in Hamlet, but I couldn't concentrate. What I really wanted was to talk to Soph, but her cell was off and her landline kept going to voice mail. I went out the back and waved at Mom.

"Hi," she said, the brim of her hat hiding her face. "When did you get in?"

"Early. I left Soph's about six."

Mom didn't have a clue when I'd got home. With Jordie at Dad's, she'd stayed at Damon's. I heard her car pull up about nine. I like Damon. He's not bad for an old guy. He's got a kid too, called India, who's a bit younger than Jordie, and whenever Damon has her, she and Jordie get on really well. They make a nice little family unit, the four of them.

I drifted around, not really knowing what I was doing. I tried to get my homework done, but I couldn't stop thinking about the weekend and how much my life had turned around in forty-eight hours. I moved from room to room, touching photos and ornaments, aware of how normal everything felt. At last I got through to Sophie.

"What've you been doing? Why weren't you answering your phone?"

"Been busy," she said so softly I could hardly hear her, "on the Net."

"How'd you get home?"

"Bus." She sounded really weird and kind of flat.

"Are you all right? Was Glenn with you?" I hoped he hadn't left her on her own. Maybe she was pissed off at me for leaving her.

"Yeah." She went silent for a while.

"Where did you go?" Something was up. It sounded like she didn't want to talk. I was busting to tell her my news, but I couldn't because something wasn't right.

"Glenn's place."

"Just the two of you?"

"Some of his friends were there too."

"Oh," I laughed, "bit of a party, hey?" I wanted her to get happy. I wanted to tell her about Lewis.

"Something like that," she said, but she sounded like she was about to cry. "Mia, I don't want to get separated from you ever again when we go out." She was verging on hysterics.

"Sophie, what is it? Did something happen?"

"No, no, I'm fine," she said, but I knew she was lying.

"Bullshit," I said. "What happened?"

"Nothing, honest," her voice was almost normal again. "Anyway, how'd it go with Lewis?"

"Yeah, good," I said. I didn't want to tell her now. I needed her to be in the right mood and focused on the job of analyzing the whole situation for me. "I'll tell you about it later."

"Oh, right!" She sounded like she knew anyway. "I'll catch you tomorrow."

The rest of the day dragged on. By five I was feeling flat. I had no energy to do anything. I couldn't concentrate, and when I lay down I couldn't sleep. Mom was still working in the garden, proving she could do everything, including mow the lawn. Jordie wasn't home yet, and I had nothing to do except my English assignment. I ended up putting together a really pathetic effort, but hopefully there'd be time before class to fix it up.

Dad dropped Jordie off but didn't come in to see me. I watched his car pull out of the driveway. Was he sulking because I'd rejected him for a better option? Tough. He could be a real pain like that.

I sat at my desk writing Lewis's initials over and over, linking them with my own. Mom opened my door and I quickly covered up the paper.

"Dinner's ready," she said. "It's tacos."

Tacos are Jordie's favorite. Mom always makes our favorite food after we've been at Dad's.

"Thought you did homework all night?" she said, looking at my files.

"Yeah," I said, "but we slacked off a bit early and didn't really finish."

"Mia," Mom looked annoyed, "if you're not getting your homework done, you can forget about staying out till all hours of the night."

"Yeah, yeah," I said.

sophie

The note in my locker from Dominic inviting me and Mia to his birthday was typical Dom. He was always nice to Mia, including her in things we did; he treated her like a little sister. I think she was a tiny bit in love with him.

"Don't you want to go?" she asked me in math.

It had been a couple of months since I'd split with Dom, and I'd withdrawn from the social scene again. I hadn't gone out with any other guys. I couldn't—they weren't Dominic. And I couldn't face him. I know he felt terrible about our breakup and thought it was all his fault. It was like payback time for all my stupidity. And unless I told him the truth, there was nothing I could say to convince him otherwise, so I did my best to avoid him. Our school is so big it wasn't hard to take a different route if I saw him from a distance. And even though I really wanted to go to his party, I'd heard he was going out with Karen Baxter, and it would kill me to see him with her. I'd already decided the pain wouldn't be worth it.

"Come on," Mia said encouragingly.

Mia was desperate for a boyfriend. All she wanted was to meet someone. So despite myself I said, "Okay, let's do it."

I managed to get quite enthusiastic about Mia's debut, though I didn't know how I was going to handle being in the same room as Dom again. Of course, I saw him the minute we entered the party. I chugged my vodka, and with a reminder to myself not to get too plastered, I walked straight up to him. *Face the fear head on.* Immediately, I felt it emanating from him in waves: he still wanted me. I think I might have made up with him there and then, forced myself to be truthful. But Karen was standing next to him like she owned him. I'm not the aggressive sort, and Karen is a really nice girl, but I swear I could've smashed her in the face. She was so possessive, putting her hand on his arm.

He's mine, I wanted to scream, but I couldn't because

Sophie "Einstein" Spencer had given him up.

Mom had always told me I could be good at whatever I really applied myself to, and she was right. I had become great at being someone else. I could deceive everyone around me, even those who loved me and knew me. I was a top-notch actress. I could hide any emotion, assume any feeling or personality trait. You want happy? Watch my eyes light up. You want sympathy? No one can beat my listening and empathizing skills. So if Karen Baxter was so insecure she had to assert her place, fine. I headed off with Mia to have some fun and prove to the world that I didn't need Dominic Cimino.

Sometimes things don't work out the way you want, though. Every now and then I'd steal a glance at Dom and catch him looking my way. You'd think that would've made me happy, but it didn't. It made me feel worse.

And then there was Mia. I had the best time with her, but when things didn't go her way she could be a real sulker. Around me, Mia in her comfort zone was outgoing and funny, but when she was under pressure she shut right down. Or she got defensive and demanding.

We'd been watching the crowd, trying to pretend we were having a good time, but the music was awful, the drinks were warm, and everyone else seemed to be having a better time. She wasn't getting into the scene, and I was too preoccupied with Dominic to be any help. So, despite my vow to make this night about Mia, I didn't. A girl she knew turned up, and I took the opportunity to escape for a second. I love her, but in a mood like this she was too much like hard work.

I slipped out the back and ran straight into Dom.

"Whatchya doing?" he asked.

There seemed so many possible answers to that question, but all I said was, "Getting some air."

"I know what you mean." He took a step closer, slurring slightly. "Soph?"

"Dom?"

He grabbed my hand and pulled me close. My heart was hammering against my rib cage. "I've got a girlfriend," he said.

Even though he wasn't telling me anything I didn't know, it felt like a smack in the face. But I just smiled at him.

"I really want to kiss you," he said, "but that's not fair on, um …"

"Karen?" I offered.

"Yeah, Karen." He looked around. "Karen. Yeah, she's real nice, you know."

I didn't want to hear it. I knew she was nice. And beautiful too. I pulled my hand away and said, as meanly as I could, "Then you'd better find her. If she's so nice she doesn't need to be cheated on," and I turned and left him standing there.

I stumbled across Lewis Scott in a quiet part of the garden, hanging out with a few of his friends. Lewis was totally hot. He had it all: looks, personality, and money. He was also Mia's dream guy.

"Hey, Lewis, what are you doing out here?" I asked, jumping into social butterfly mode.

"I've got something." He waved me over and opened his hand. "Want one?"

"What are they? Es?"

"Yep."

"How many can you spare?" I asked.

I woke up for school feeling really flat. After being so high all weekend I'd suddenly crashed. I shut my eyes and tried to think about Lewis and how good my life was. But a dark cloud had settled over my head. I wondered if I was getting my period—and then the thought of that made me aware of exactly what I'd done. I'd had unprotected sex!

The realization took my breath away. I put my head in my hands, trying to control the rising sense of panic. How could I have been so dumb? When we were in the back of his car it had occurred to me, but I didn't know what to say. I was too embarrassed to ask if he had a condom. I thought he might've brought one out. And when he didn't, I didn't want to spoil the moment. After that, I didn't give it any more thought. Oh shit!

I freaked out. I paced madly around the room, my heart hammering. Surely he would have had condoms. I should have said something. Oh God, how could I have been so stupid?

I didn't want to go to school. I was sure I must be pregnant.

In the shower I watched the water run over my flat stomach. Please, please, please, don't let me be pregnant. I knew from sex ed that you only had to do it once. What had I done?

I slipped into the kitchen.

"Morning," Mom said, getting herself a coffee.

I kept my head down. I didn't want to talk. I was afraid I would cry. I poured a juice and unthinkingly left the fridge door open.

"Hello, Mia. Hello, Mother," she said loudly and sarcastically. She always had to jump on me the minute I did something she didn't like. I sighed loudly and stared at her. Why did she have to start the day like this?

"Hello, Mother."

"I don't like your tone," she snapped. "And is it so hard to put things away and shut the damn fridge door?" She picked up the juice and slammed the fridge door shut. She was brewing up a fight.

"Whatever," I said, taking a piece of toast out the front door with me.

I didn't see Sophie when I first got to school, and she's not in my homeroom. I didn't want to talk to anyone else and I felt like crying. What if I was pregnant? It was all I could think about. Pregnant, dropping out of school, having to go on welfare, miserable and lonely. I'd ruined everything.

Finally, at lunch, I found Soph sitting alone on our bench. She looked as depressed as I felt.

"What's up?" I asked.

"Nothing," she said, not meeting my eyes. And I could tell there was something seriously wrong.

"Sure, Soph." I was scratching at the wooden bench with a pen. "What's the matter with you?"

"Tired, I guess. It was a big weekend." Her voice was so odd.

"What happened at Glenn's?"

"Nothing," she said abruptly and looked down.

We were silent. I didn't have the energy to force it out of her if she didn't want to talk.

"What about you?" she asked, looking down at my scratching—it was a butterfly.

The words hurtled out: I'd had sex with the most

popular guy in school and I might be pregnant. I waited for her to speak.

"You need the morning-after pill," she said matter-of-factly. "It's a bit late. You need to take it as soon as you can. But if it's within seventy-two hours it should be okay."

"Mom can't know," I said.

"She doesn't have to. You can get it at a pharmacy." She looked at her watch. "Let's skip math and do it now."

I looked at her gratefully. "Thanks, Soph." If I could make sure I wasn't pregnant, I'd never make the same mistake again.

"Don't stress out," she said and smiled like she'd seen it all before. "You won't be pregnant."

And isn't it funny, because when she said it, I believed her.

I felt so stupid explaining to the pharmacist that I'd had unprotected sex, but he didn't give me a hard time. He asked if I'd taken the morning-after pill before and warned me it could make me feel a bit ill. If I vomited it up I'd have to take another one. He asked if I wanted to take it now. I nodded. I'd have to take another one exactly twelve hours later, which would make it one o'clock in the morning. I looked around nervously, hoping no one I knew, or who knew my mom, would see me. He gave me a glass of water and I swallowed the pill there, in the middle of the pharmacy, right behind the Lancôme counter.

We sat in the park afterwards. I felt even worse than when I'd woken up.

"I feel so …" I struggled to explain myself, "… depressed, I guess."

"Yeah," she nodded. "Maybe it's the comedown. You know, after feeling so high, I guess you crash a bit later."

"Maybe." But I was thinking about Lewis. I couldn't focus on anything but him. Now I was scared that he'd think I'd been too easy. He hadn't called me on Sunday. I thought part of my mood was probably to do with that. I'd considered texting him, but I didn't want him to think I was desperate. He had to call me first. I hadn't seen him at school either, and his car wasn't in the parking lot. And now I'd taken this massive dose of hormones in the hope I wouldn't have to have an abortion later.

I was starting to feel a bit stupid.

sophie

Ecstasy is the word. And before Dom's party that was all it was to us. Just a word. It was something we knew other kids did. Something Mia and I had said we'd probably try. The way people spoke about it made it sound so amazing—magical even. And it was partly curiosity that made me take that first step. Mia was sulking, Dom was with Karen, I felt terrible, and Lewis had the means. I was in a kind of what-have-I-got-to-lose mood. And the answer was: absolutely nothing. But, as it turned out, I couldn't have been more wrong.

Anyway, that night it was fantastic. It was like I'd woken up. All of a sudden I had so much energy. I wanted to talk and I wanted to dance. I wanted to find out everything there was to know about everyone. I was filled with the greatest sense of peace and unity. I watched Mia relax back into herself and I felt carried away with the wildest sensations. And I found Dominic again.

By this stage he was drunk. Totally wasted. Karen was asleep, and he was sitting on his own, a bottle of vodka in his hands. I sat down next to him. I felt like I was buzzing, and I put my hand on his leg. I loved the feel of him. I wanted him back and that was what I wanted to say.

He tried to sit up. "I love you, Sophie," he said, before he slumped against me. "I really, really love you."

"Dom, it's okay," I began, but he was sitting up now and had hold of my hands. He was trying as hard as he could to act sober. Because he's so serious about his football training I'd never seen him even slightly drunk before. He was wrecked.

"You need to know how sorry I am." He squeezed my hands hard. "I'm so sorry for what I did to you."

"Dom, you didn't do anything." Kind and beautiful Dom. I loved him more then than ever. "You don't have to be sorry. It's okay."

"It's *not*," he said loudly. "It's not. And I can't forgive myself." He staggered to his feet. I jumped up and put an arm around him, he was so unsteady. "Beautiful Sophie," he hugged me hard. And at that moment all I wanted was for him to hug me forever. "I never deserved you. I'm so sorry."

And he walked off, slightly sideways, but with enough forward momentum to make it into the house. I watched him go, feeling full of love for him. It seemed like everything would work out, like everything would be sweet.

Lewis dropped us home. Mia was in total heaven. I watched her float away every time he looked at her and I was really happy for her. I don't think she knew how beautiful she was. After the foul mood she'd been in, the ecstasy brought out the very best in her. It didn't surprise me one bit that Lewis wanted to see her again. She glowed, and she'd been so funny. This was the Mia I loved so much. So when I got home, the whole thing seemed like a really huge success. Our first ecstasy experience. I was filled with the most positive feelings that things would work out for me and Dom and that Mia would finally have the boyfriend she had dreamed of.

I went to modeling that morning with a huge smile that nothing seemed able to erase. All day I thought about what I was going to do. I wanted to come clean with

Dom. I was sure he, more than anyone else, would understand me.

Poor Dom. He would've woken up with a massive hangover—when I left he was passed out on the couch in the games room. He looked so peaceful. I checked no one was looking and then leaned over and kissed him. He didn't even stir, he was so out of it.

So I really didn't want to go to the dance party that night. By the time Mia texted me I was feeling pretty wrecked. I just wanted to stay home. But when she texted me back, so desperate, I had to give in. This was her big chance. So I agreed to go, and part of me was hopeful that the next weekend it would be Mia and Lewis, and me and Dominic.

I said it before: things don't always work out the way you want. When Lewis offered me ecstasy again I thought about them being made in someone's backyard lab. I imagined some big, fat, sweaty guy mashing chemicals together while a cigarette dangled from his lips. They could have anything in them. That thought alone really scared me. And that's another difference between me and Mia—I'm a lot more cautious. I weigh up the risks, I think ahead. Mia jumps in feet first and freaks about the consequences later. But I didn't want to draw attention to myself, and Mia had already taken one, so I swallowed it. But I promised myself even then, before any of the bad stuff happened, that I wouldn't take another for a really long time.

Something else I ignored was my initial impression of Glenn. At first I thought he was pretty sleazy, and I chatted to him non-stop just to keep him at a distance. Once the E kicked in I didn't mind him so much. I convinced myself he was just different.

We lost Mia and Lewis pretty early in the night. The place was packed, and I clung on to Glenn, frightened of being left completely alone. The E was as good as the night before, and Glenn and I danced for hours. He couldn't keep his hands off me, but I didn't mind. With the drugs and the music I was back in the peace, love, and unity zone.

Then we went outside for air and water and saw that Lewis's car had gone. I had a momentary feeling of panic about Mia, but then I figured she'd be okay. Lewis would be looking after her.

"Shall we walk to the bus stop?" Glenn suggested. I nodded and let him hold my hand as we walked along.

We were the only two on the bus and we talked all the way to his stop. He had an arm around me, but he knew we were platonic. I wasn't interested in him at all. In fact, all I talked about was Dominic and what an idiot I'd been to split up with him.

"Hey, come to my place and I'll drive you home," he said when we reached his bus stop. I considered it for a second. It was five more stops until the city, where I had to transfer, and then a short walk home. I'd be alone, but the streets were well lit and there's transit security. I shook my head.

"Nah, I'll stay on. Thanks anyway. Great night."

He stood with his hand holding the door from shutting. The bus was about to leave. "I can't let you ride on your own," he said. "I'll stay with you and catch the next bus back again."

I shook my head, genuinely surprised at his gesture. "No, Glenn, this is probably the last one. You might not get back."

"I'll walk then." He took his hand away. The door started to close.

I jumped up from the seat. I couldn't let him do that. "No." I pressed the button to open the doors again. "I'll come."

mia

The week passed painfully slowly. I had to wait to see if my period came. The morning-after pill had made me nauseous, but I hadn't vomited. I prayed daily that it had worked. Lewis didn't call, and I became a serial phone checker. At school I'd walk through the cafeteria inconspicuously, sneaking furtive glances toward the grade twelve group, but I never saw him there. And as the days passed with no word, I gradually realized the harsh truth. I'd been just a fling for him, a fifteen-year-old virgin to take out, get wasted, and screw.

I was miserable, and Soph had been down all week too. I wanted her to reassure me that sleeping with Lewis had been the right thing to do, and that no, I wasn't a slut, but she didn't get into it, and I couldn't understand why not. I thought about all the hours I'd spent listening to her when she had a new guy.

She was so distant. Something was definitely up. I'd

heard that Dominic and Karen had split up after the party. Karen was pretty embarrassed about getting so hammered. And I'd seen Dominic and Soph talking at school, but Soph wouldn't talk to me about that either.

"He just needs a friend," was all she'd say. I was feeling left out and let down.

I figured Soph must be embarrassed about Glenn. The guys she's been with before–with the obvious exception of Thomas Creep Westcroft–were all way nicer than him. I wanted her to open up about it–she'd begun to once, but then closed down. If I could only get her to talk, I knew I could make her feel better. And then everything would go back to normal.

"Do you want to talk about Glenn?" I asked her gently one day.

She straightened and looked me dead in the eyes. "There's nothing else to say," she said in a hard voice.

"But, Soph, maybe you need to." I was trying to reassure her that I was okay about it, but I got the impression she was scared of being judged.

Then she put her hand up and said, "I don't want to talk about it. Just drop it." And she walked off.

I've never felt this way about her before, but I actually thought she was being a total bitch.

Friday morning I woke with a dull ache in my lower back. I nearly screamed with joy. I've never been so excited to have my period before. I stood under the hot water in the shower and cried. Thank God for that. I promised myself I'd go on the pill before I'd ever take such a stupid risk again. I still had a life in front of me.

Things just kept getting better. As I got dressed for school my cell beeped at me: Message Received. I opened the inbox. When I read the number, my stomach started flipping out. It was Lewis.

sorry been sic much betta now cum to party tonite?

I felt the smile stretching to my ears. He'd been sick and off school! I immediately texted him back, my thumbs flying over the keys.

abso-fkn-lutely! wot time?

As I pressed Send I realized how desperate that would look. I wished I could take it back. I sat on the edge of my bed feeling my ears burn. I'd just made myself look like a complete and utter loser. Then my phone beeped again. He was one fast texter.

fantastic pic u up at 7 soph 2?

Relieved and happy he'd said "fantastic," I quickly

messaged Soph. She texted back straightaway.

cant got stuff on tlk @ skool.

I'd known she'd say no. Something was so wrong with her. It was like how she acted after Thomas Westcroft–alienating herself, becoming anti-social. But I had to go, even without her. I texted Lewis back.

S no but c u @7

Mom was in the kitchen putting things in the dishwasher.

"Hello," I said cheerfully.

She looked at me suspiciously. "What's going on? Why are you so happy?"

"Can I go out tonight?"

"Oh, who with?" Mom asked.

"Lewis Scott," I said proudly.

"Really?" Mom said, sitting down. "Who's he then?"

"Just, like, the most popular guy in the world." I had the biggest grin on my face. "He wants to take me to a party."

"Do I get to meet him?" Mom asked.

"Mom, if you say one thing to embarrass me, I'll kill you."

I was preoccupied all day with what I was going to wear. When I asked Soph what she was doing instead of coming to the party, she was evasive and changed the subject. And then it occurred to me that I might be wrong about her. It felt crazy even to think this, but could Sophie be jealous of me? I had Lewis, and she'd ended up with Glenn. If that's how it was, I was glad she wasn't coming.

I spent ages getting ready. The black pants made my thighs look fat, and the red top made me look completely flat-chested. I needed a push-up bra. In the end I settled for a pink halter-neck and three-quarter denim jeans. I just had to get some new clothes. It took me an hour to do my hair, but when I'd finished I had supermodel straightness. Looking in the mirror at the end result, I relaxed slightly. It wasn't too bad.

Waiting for Lewis was nerve-racking. What if he didn't show up? What if he changed his mind and took someone else? Mom was sitting with me in the TV room and I tried to stop looking out the window. We both drank a glass of wine, even though Mom gave me her standard lecture on moderation and made me promise not to drink while I was out.

I promised. "Just water, Mom, honest," and chugged my wine. What if he'd forgotten about me?

"You look beautiful." Mom was acting like the proud mother witnessing her daughter's first date. If she knew we'd already bonked she would have dropped dead.

At last I heard the low grumble of his car. I sat as calmly as I could, listening to the thud of his feet across the driveway. I felt like vomiting. Mom jumped up and winked at me as she went to open the door.

"Hello," she said, offering him her hand. "I'm Rae."

He shook it, smiling at her, and looked over her shoulder at me. I hoped my face wasn't red, but I did feel embarrassed. And it wasn't because of Mom—actually I thought it was pretty cool she'd used her first name. I was just embarrassed about him being in my house, not because there's anything wrong with our house but just because it was him—hot Lewis, in my house, meeting my mom, about to take me out.

He almost filled the doorway, he was so tall.

"Does she have to be home at a certain time?" he asked, mega-politely, grabbing my hand. I stood next to him, my head level with his shoulder, my hand not too sweaty in his.

"As long as it's reasonable," Mom said. She was clearly impressed and not wanting to come across like a control freak. "Have a great time. Drive carefully."

"Of course, ma'am," he said, and I almost choked. Ma'am. What was he trying to prove?

He opened the passenger door and I slid into the seat. Mom was still watching from the house, smiling and looking relieved that such a polite and trustworthy guy was taking me out. I waved at her as Lewis started the engine and reversed out of the driveway.

I didn't know what to say to him, so I laughed at his try-hard act. "You definitely impressed my mom," I said, watching him.

The corner of his mouth lifted into a smile. "It never hurts to have the mother onside," he said with a wink.

"So where are we going?" I asked.

"A friend of mine, Tower, is having a party," Lewis said, pulling into the parking lot of a deserted shopping center. "You won't know anyone–these guys aren't at school. But don't worry, they're all really cool."

I suddenly felt way out of my depth. I wouldn't know anyone but Lewis. I felt slightly sick.

"Let's drop these now and they'll be hitting when we get there," he said, holding out a couple of pills. These were a dark pink, almost magenta, with the picture of an apple stamped into the surface. I picked one out of his hand, trying to smile confidently. All week when I hadn't heard from him I'd beaten myself up thinking he'd found me too easy. Obviously I'd been wrong. As I looked at his smiling face I knew that he did want to be with me. And the E would make it all perfect.

As he drove, Lewis explained that his family used to live in the south end of the city and that he and Tower had been friends since grade school. After Lewis moved they still played on the same football team and got together on weekends. Tower had dropped out of school after grade eleven. His parents had bought him a furniture shop to run and his own house to live in.

"So then he employed people to run it—Tower doesn't like to work too hard, might interfere with his social life. Normally he goes in a couple of times a week, makes sure everyone's doing their job, takes a bit of cash, and blows it in a weekend."

"So what's the occasion?" I asked. Lewis and his friends seemed so sophisticated. They had money and freedom. It was like being on some TV show, with hot guys and fast cars.

"It's the weekend," Lewis said, laughing. "That's always an occasion to celebrate."

By the time we arrived at Tower's place I was starting to loosen up. His house was on a massive block, lit up with flashing party lights. The Raconteurs blasted from the back garden.

There were so many people in the house and backyard that I hung on to Lewis tightly. A DJ had set up in the corner and was professionally mixing the records. As I felt the beat begin to surge through me, a huge, red-faced guy appeared. Next to him, even Lewis looked short.

"Hey, Tower," Lewis shouted as they clapped each other hard on the back. "How you doin'?"

"Good," Tower replied, eyeing me as I swayed and tapped my foot to the rhythm. "Who's this?"

"Mia," I said, offering my hand and smiling at him.

"Hi, Mia." He squeezed my hand tightly. "Watch this boy, he's bad news."

"Piss off," Lewis said good-naturedly.

Tower was loud and animated. He turned everything into a joke. And he was like a magnet. The crowd around him grew as he threw his arms around telling some story about a friend of his who would only marry a girl who was a pure blonde. When he came to the punch line everyone was roaring with laughter, Tower the loudest. Finally Lewis grabbed my arm and dragged me to a quieter corner.

"Tower'll go on like that for hours," he said, finding us a bottle of water.

"He's funny," I said.

"He's always been funny. He's famous for his practical jokes." Lewis dragged me down next to him and told me stories about the stuff he and Tower used to get up to when they were kids. I listened, watching his gorgeous face, knowing I could reach over and touch him if I wanted to. Which I did. I felt beautiful and amazingly confident. I knew Lewis wanted me as much as I wanted him. And I could tell him things too. He listened to me talk about Sophie and about Mom and Dad—not too much, I didn't want to bring up the depressing stuff.

By about eleven I felt myself coming down. I'd lost the beat and the rhythm. Everything was suddenly flat.

"I don't think these are much good," Lewis said apologetically. "Let's have another one."

I put out my hand. I didn't want to drift out of it while everyone else was still rolling. The second one kicked in quicker and kept me going until four in the morning, when we finally left the party.

sophie

Glenn lived in a part of town I wasn't familiar with. As the brightly lit stop fell behind us, the dark, shifting shapes of the neighborhood started to fill me with unease. It was an inner-city suburb with dirty shopfronts covered in graffiti, cracked pavements, and derelict houses. At this time of night there were few people out. I tightened my grip on Glenn's hand.

"Through here," he said, leading me down a narrow alley lit only by the crescent of the moon. I stepped over smashed bottles and rubbish, clear-headed now. The E had worn off, taking with it the last feelings of peacefulness. Now a sense of claustrophobia rose up in my chest. Finally we came out near the banks of the river, and in the darkness I heard the soft lapping of water. I breathed deeply, relieved to be out in the open again, and smelled the overwhelming pong of algae.

"Ewww," I said, grabbing my nose.

Glenn laughed and dragged me along. "I pay higher rent for the luxury of smelling the river."

His place was in a stack of apartments, most with their lights off. We walked up the steps and suddenly I wondered what the hell I was doing. I clutched my bag tighter, fighting off a sense of panic. I didn't know Glenn, I didn't know him at all. But he was opening the door, and as I stood on the threshold, I reminded myself he was Lewis Scott's friend. It'd be okay.

Inside, party lights flashed, and to my surprise there were a couple of guys sitting on the sofa.

"Hey," one of them said, looking up with an apathetic expression.

"Hey," I said, smiling to hide my sudden rush of nerves.

"Want a drink?" Glenn asked, unscrewing the cap of a rum bottle.

"Nah." I shifted nervously on the doorstep. "I really should get going, you know."

"I'll get my keys. Here, you must be thirsty," Glenn handed me a rum and Coke. "I'll just be a sec."

I held the glass in my hands, suddenly realizing I was thirsty. I told myself to relax. I wasn't sure what the vibe was, but there was no need to panic. So I sat on the edge of the sofa and tried to make conversation, but the guys weren't very forthcoming. They seemed pretty out of it. I sipped my drink as I waited for Glenn to get his keys.

A strange feeling had begun to creep through my body. My head felt fuzzy. I didn't want to drink anymore. I craned my head around to look for Glenn. He seemed to have been gone a very long time.

My eyes snapped open as the back of my head hit the wall. Glenn was holding me against it, his breath hot in my face, his tongue shoved wetly into my mouth. I recoiled. I couldn't keep my eyes open even though each time he hoisted me up my head thudded against the wall.

I tried to speak, but the words wouldn't come out.

"C'mon, Soph," Glenn was biting my neck and his hands were under my top. He grabbed my breasts painfully and I screamed. I tried to push him off, but I was too weak. My arms flopped uselessly. My head was swimming. My vision was cloudy. Everything was gray. I needed control. I didn't know what was happening.

Next time I opened my eyes I was on the floor, looking at the foot of a bed. I sat up slowly. My neck ached painfully. A plastic wrapper was stuck to my cheek. It rustled, but I couldn't move it. I grabbed the bed and pulled myself up. It was a tangle of filthy sheets. I was alone. There was the taste of blood in my mouth. My heart was racing. I stood up and had to grab the wall for support. My head swam and my breath was coming in shallow gasps. I was filled with overwhelming terror. I had no idea what had happened. I felt my body. I was fully dressed. My shoes were still on.

I staggered to the door and peered into the other room. Glenn and one of the other guys were sitting on the couch, facing away from me. They couldn't see me. Fear made my body shake violently. I clamped my teeth together tightly to stop them chattering. The front door was open. I tried to move silently, but every noise seemed magnified a thousand times.

I took some deep breaths and tried to feel some control, but my body wasn't responding well. My head thumped and my neck screamed in pain. I had to get out. I knew Glenn would stop me. I inhaled and ran. Past my bag, past the couch, straight into a screen door. I hit the mesh at full force and bounced backward.

I staggered forward again, trying to keep my footing, terrified. Behind me was the sound of laughter.

"You gotta open the door first."

My hands trembled as I turned the handle. I expected to feel his hand on my shoulder. Nausea filled my throat. But I managed to open the door and stagger out. Cold wind hit my face and blew my hair into my eyes. The steps down looked too long and steep. I clutched the railing tightly.

"Sophie." Glenn almost sang my name. I was shaking uncontrollably. He was right behind me. My vision doubled, and I felt myself rocking, about to fall. He was coming out. I tried not to panic. I edged one foot off the top step.

"Here!" My bag hit me in the back of the head, knocking me off the step. My ankle twisted underneath me and I went down, still holding the railing.

"Watch your step," he laughed, swinging the door shut.

He was gone.

I had to get home. The idea of home filled me with tears. I limped down the stairs and picked my bag up. I looked around, confused and terrified. I had to walk back up the alley, past the derelict stores and druggies and rapists. I couldn't do it. Everything was menacing. I hobbled to a street light. I wanted to call my mom, but the face of my cell showed 3:30 a.m. I held it tightly in my hands. I looked back toward the alley and Glenn's apartment, then I started walking in the opposite direction, Glenn's laughter still echoing in my ears. Through the shadows I walked and walked. Up ahead were stores. And on the other side of the road a brightly lit fast food restaurant with people moving around inside. I whimpered in relief as I limped closer to the light and the people, flipped open my phone, and pressed D. I prayed as I listened to it ring that he would pick up.

mia

When I got up on Saturday afternoon Mom was waiting for me in the kitchen, wanting to hear all the details. She seemed pretty excited, and not annoyed with me for sleeping away most of the day.

"What time did you get in?" she asked. I figured it was a test. She and Damon had stayed home—she'd probably been awake. I didn't want her to catch me out in a lie.

"About four," I said. "I'm really sorry, but we had no idea of the time. It was just such a great night and Lewis and I were talking so much we didn't know how late it was."

She frowned. "Yeah, well—don't make it a habit. Four is too late—even on the weekend." She put a cup of coffee in front of me. "So tell me, what happened?"

Later that day Lewis messaged me.

my house tonite U & me Pic u up @ 6

I texted him back immediately.

C U soon

Mom didn't mind at all when I told her I was going to Lewis's for dinner. She liked the way he called her ma'am. She saw him as perfect boyfriend material.

Lewis pulled up in front of his amazing Mediterranean-style home overlooking the beach. The sky above the ocean was a swirl of pink and blue. I walked up the footpath to the front door, two steps behind him, gawking at everything. He disarmed the security system and flung the door open wide.

"Come in," he said, grabbing my hand and pulling me into the gigantic entrance hall.

The kitchen was the size of a small apartment—my mom would have been in heaven. They had a fridge you could walk into and a pantry larger than our bathroom. Lewis made rum and Cokes. I'd drunk more in this last week than the whole of my life. I sipped at it as he showed me through the rest of the house. They had a theater room like a small cinema, with twinkling lights recessed into the ceiling and walls draped in heavy velvet curtains. The screen filled an entire wall.

I followed Lewis, making the right noises, but to tell the truth, I was completely overwhelmed. I knew people lived like this, but I'd never experienced it before. His bedroom was massive, with its own bathroom, of course. I sat on his double bed and smelled his aftershave. The walls were covered with pictures of half-dressed women wrapped in gleaming pythons or straddling motorbikes, and there was a huge black entertainment system. Everything was so sophisticated.

"I'll make you dinner," he said, draining the last of his drink. I perched on a stool in the kitchen trying to find things to say. I hated the awkwardness. After everything we'd done together I couldn't believe I still found it so difficult just to sit and talk to him.

He pulled his plastic bag of pills out and I felt a rush of relief. Call it psychological, but knowing I'd have a little assistance helped me drop the anxiety that had been building from the minute he unlocked the front door. We each took an E, and I propped my elbows on the bench and watched him cook. He was unbelievable! Not only a sex god but a chef too. He made a pasta sauce and passed me things to chop as he stirred the pot.

"So, where are your parents?" I asked, sipping my rum and giving him what I hoped was a sexy look.

"China," he said, throwing a handful of basil into the pot and turning the heat down. "They export timber there and have the locals make it into furniture, which they import back in. Saves heaps of money in labor and increases their profit margin. They left two weeks ago and won't be back for months."

"Really?" I said, following him out back to an enormous swimming pool that glowed iridescent blue in the night. Across its surface fingers of steam danced upward into the light. I kicked my shoes off and stuck a toe in. The water was hot. "Do you often stay on your own?"

"Yeah." He pulled out a chair for me and we sat opposite each other. "For the last couple of years I've basically been here by myself. Before that I had a nanny. A short, hairy Polish woman who barely spoke English and gave me lots of candies. When I was ten she used to warn me my tits would fall out."

"Your tits?" I said incredulously.

"Yeah. It was a while before I figured out she meant my teeth. When I turned fourteen they figured I was old enough to look after myself."

"You've been doing this since you were fourteen?"

"Yeah. It's good. There's a woman who comes in and cleans and stuff." He stood up. "Let's have dinner and then a swim."

Even though his cooking smelled fantastic, I didn't really want to eat. Sucking up pasta and flicking red sauce over my face would be a complete turnoff. Also, I think maybe the E suppressed my appetite. He dished me up a huge bowlful, which I pushed around with my fork. I didn't want to offend him, but I didn't want to look bloated in my suit either.

"Not hungry?" he asked.

"It's fantastic," I said enthusiastically, "but no, not really."

"That's okay. Leave it. Maybe we'll have it for breakfast."

He was inviting me to stay the night.

While he mixed more drinks I phoned Mom. I stood out on the balcony, the sea and sky now blended together into a wall of inky blackness streaked by glittering shards of stars. I listened to the invisible surf as her cell rang.

"Hello?" She was out with Damon. There was the sound of tinkling glasses, muted chatter, and piano music. My guess was she was at the Mint Leaf. "Everything all right?"

"Yeah, fine," I said quickly. "You at dinner?"

"Mint Leaf."

"Thought so. Lewis's parents have invited me to stay the night," I lied, and then quickly added, "in the guest room, of course."

"Of course," Mom said. "That's fine. Thanks for calling, honey. See you in the morning."

When I walked back through the floating white curtain Lewis smiled. "Swim?"

"Sure." I changed into my bathing suit and didn't waste time assessing myself in the mirror of his bathroom. His shirt was lying on the floor. I picked it up and breathed it in. It smelled like Lewis, warm and heavenly.

He was sitting in the hot tub. I dropped my towel and he watched me as I walked toward him. I felt like a swimsuit model. He took my hand and helped me down into the pool. It was warm and bubbly. I sat back, mindful of my hair. It was like I was living someone else's life.

Later, in his room, I was too embarrassed to tell him I had my period. I quickly changed and then pushed him down onto the bed. He seemed to like me being in control. I took away his towel and peeled off his boardshorts. He lay back against the bed with his eyes shut and I ran my fingernails across his body and followed them with light kisses. He was at my mercy, and moaned every time my lips touched his body. I knew what to do; Soph had told me enough about it. And it was weird, but it wasn't as bad as she'd said. When he was done I rocked back on my heels watching him. His eyes were still shut and he was completely relaxed.

"Come here, babe," he said, opening his eyes slightly. I felt totally happy as he pulled me in to his side. And it was like that we ended up going to sleep.

sophie

Dom came to get me. And he was mad as hell. I'd never, ever seen him mad before, not even slightly aggressive. When he found me I'd managed to tidy up a bit. I spat on a tissue and wiped the mascara streaks from my face, brushed my hair, and calmed down a bit. I'd vomited in the gutter, violent, heaving spasms that left me feeling weak and empty. I tried to figure out what had happened, but my head was cloudy and the thoughts literally whizzed through my brain. Terror kept rising up, even though I couldn't piece anything together. At the sight of his car I broke into a fresh flood of tears. I knew he was mad before he even spoke, he slammed the door of his car so hard.

"Who the fuck is he?" he said as he squatted down beside me.

"No," I shook my head. "Don't."

"The fucking prick." Dom put his arms around me. "I'll kill him."

I buried my face into the warmth of his shirt and cried harder. He held me tightly. "Get me out of here, please," I begged.

When I woke the room was bright and warm. I sat up and my head pounded. I opened the door and peered down the hallway. No one home. I walked through the shiny kitchen, which smelled like Mr. Clean. Through the glass doors I saw Dom cleaning the pool: twist and scoop. He must have felt me watching because he looked up and gestured me toward him. I slid the door open and stepped into the sunlight.

"How're you feeling?"

Devastated. Lucky. Terrified. Relieved. I couldn't put it into words. As I pictured that apartment my heart began to race. I couldn't believe I'd made it out of there alive. "There are some things I've got to tell you," I said as he put the pool scoop down.

"Did he force you?" His eyes were fixed on mine. His hold on my hand tightened. He was furious.

"Yes, no—he didn't rape me, if that's what you

mean." I licked my lip, it was slightly swollen and felt bruised. Had he hit me? I didn't think so. "No, he tried to get me to …" I shuddered at the image of him grabbing hold of the back of my neck, forcing my head down. "He was trying to make me … do stuff. But I couldn't. I kept passing out."

"We have to go to the cops."

"No, Dom, please don't. I don't want to have to say it aloud to strangers." I didn't want to be judged and seen as a victim again. I couldn't believe I'd let this happen to me *again*. "I want to forget about it. Please."

He shook his head. "I won't forget about it. And I don't think you will either. Tell me what happened."

"I'm not sure. But I was totally straight when we got to his apartment. I think he must've slipped something into my drink. I've never felt so out of it."

"Rohypnol probably," Dom said. "It's a date rape drug. That's what they use."

"I guess I was lucky then." I smiled at him.

"Lucky?" He jumped up angrily. "Lucky because you didn't get raped? Fuck, Sophie, you didn't deserve any of that. That *shit*. At the moment he's the one who's lucky."

And suddenly I understood what he was saying, the

injustice of it. I hadn't lost control. Glenn had taken control away from me. "Dom," I said, grabbing his arm, "I'm okay now. Promise."

He looked at me like maybe I wasn't being honest, but then he relaxed slightly and wrapped me in his arms.

"Sure?" he whispered into my neck.

"Sure," I said. And I thought I *was* okay. Especially when he told me he'd split up with Karen. I shouldn't have felt so great about that, but it was hard not to. She broke up with him because she didn't like the way he acted around me. It was a relief to everyone. Especially me. All I could see were two words: *second chance*. The quicksand was slowly subsiding.

mia

I woke up feeling like it was Christmas. Lewis was still
asleep, his face soft in the morning light. I quickly got out
of bed and went into his bathroom to repair the damage
before he woke up and freaked out at the sight of the ugly
morning-monster. I brushed my teeth and hair and wiped
the mascara smudges from underneath my eyes. I hadn't
brought any deodorant with me, so I used his. It reminded
me of him. When I came out of the bathroom he was sitting
up in bed. He stretched and grabbed hold of my hand.

"Morning," he said, pinning me against the sheets and
kissing me. At that exact moment I fantasized that this
could be my life. Married to Lewis Scott and living in a
house like this with him. My future seemed more exciting
than I'd ever imagined.

Lewis wanted to go surfing and so I sat on the beach like

the dutiful girlfriend while he went out to tame the swell. Other girls were sitting on towels watching their boyfriends wait for the next wave. They were like a special clique. I sat a little way away from them, reading a *Cosmo* I'd found in the house. The sun was starting to scorch. Lewis had caught a couple of big waves and I was hoping he'd had enough. It was actually a bit boring watching him float out there on a piece of fiberglass, like shark bait.

"Are you with Lewis?" a tall, bony-hipped girl in a tiny string bikini asked me.

"Yeah," I said, shading my eyes against the sun to look up at her.

"You his little sister or what?" She looked back at her friends with a smirk.

"No." I didn't know what else to say. Was I his girlfriend?

He came running up from the surf like a guy in an Ironman competition, his wetsuit glistening. "Hey, had enough yet?" he asked.

String Bikini looked at him with drool practically hanging off her lips.

"Yeah," I said, getting up and brushing the sand off my bum.

"Thanks for being so patient," he said, putting a wet

arm around me. "How about I make you lunch?"

"Sounds great," I said, flicking my hair. I gave String Bikini my best effort at that look as Lewis grabbed my hand and we walked away up the beach.

Soph was waiting outside my English class on Monday. I hadn't heard from her all weekend. I was hoping she was feeling more like her old self because I couldn't wait to fill her in on all the gossip.

She interrupted me as I was describing the walk-in pantry. "Did you do more E?"

I'd deliberately left that out of the conversation. I'm not sure why. After all, it had been her idea in the first place. But I suppose I had the feeling she wouldn't like it.

"Yeah," I said quickly, "but it's cool–"

She butted in again. "Mia, you don't want to let this get out of hand."

She said it softly and like she was really worried. But I was pissed off. So it was okay for her to decide when we could do things, but if I went ahead and did something on my own, I was out of control? Where did she get off? And what was this really about anyway? Was it because for once I was the one with the rich, hot boyfriend?

"It's all fine," I said. "It's just a couple of Es. You know, they're not even addictive. It's no big deal." I left it at that. I was feeling kind of distant from her after that. She could tell, and she tried to get me talking about the weekend, acting like she was really interested and all, but I didn't want to talk about it anymore. The idea of her judging me like that really hurt.

Walking through the cafeteria at lunchtime, I saw Lewis. I didn't know what to do. Part of me thought I should go over to him and act like I belonged. I mean, after the last couple of weekends … But the other part of me, the part that would die of shame if I was rejected, kept me heading to where I knew I'd find Sophie. It was like the weekend was another world, where I was adult and sophisticated, and school was the place where I was dull and boring.

"Mia!" I thought I heard him shout my name. I was about to turn but stopped myself. It probably wasn't my name, and it definitely wouldn't have been him. I didn't want to turn and have him see me looking desperate.

"Mia!" He grabbed my elbow. "Didn't you hear me?"

I shook my head. "No, sorry. Hi."

And he kissed me right there, in front of everyone. I

119

thought my heart was going to stop. "Come and sit with me," he said, holding my hand and leading me back to the cafeteria.

I pointed toward the hallway. "Soph's waiting for me."

"Get her," he said, taking my bag off my shoulder. "Tell her to come too."

"Okay." I grinned at him and walked away, casually I hoped, though I felt like I had wooden legs.

Soph was sitting on our bench eating a bag of chips.

"Lewis wants us to join him in the cafeteria," I said, unable to curb the huge smile on my face.

"Yeah?" She put another chip in her mouth.

"Come on," I said. I was really annoyed with her. "I always go with you and sit with whoever you're seeing."

"What's that supposed to mean?" she snapped. "What are you trying to say?"

I was shocked. I wasn't trying to say anything. "God, Sophie, you know I really like Lewis. And he seems to like me. If it was you, we'd be down there right away. Now are you coming or not?" I turned to go, really upset. I did want her to come with me. I didn't want to walk back and join all those grade twelves on my own.

"Sorry," she said, jumping up and grabbing her bag. "Yeah, of course, let's go."

Thank God for Sophie; I have to forgive her for everything. She is the most socially adept person I have ever known. She walks so confidently, swinging her bag over her shoulder, smiling and saying hi to everyone. This was my turn to be the leader, but it was so automatic for me to hang back and smile from behind her.

Lewis grabbed hold of my hand. "This is Mia," he said, introducing me. "You know Soph."

Her smile faltered for a second, but then it was back as brilliant as ever. "Hi. Shift over, Ian, and let me sit down," she said, squeezing onto the bench.

Lewis was asking me what I'd been doing, but there wasn't a lot to say aside from boring schoolwork. His friend Sean started talking about catching waves and Lewis, still holding my hand, turned his attention to that.

I looked around to see what else was happening. Soph was leaning back against the wall. The top button of her shirt was undone and as she moved she was giving quick flashes of her black bra. Ian leaned in closer, his eyes fixed on her cleavage. There were a few other girls talking softly among themselves. These are the most popular girls of the school, and they always hang out together. I suddenly realized they were talking about Soph.

Kayla elbowed Justine. "Look," she whispered, pointing.

Soph was now leaning forward, and her red G-string was visible above her low-cut hipsters. She was totally unaware of the wardrobe malfunction.

The bell went, and as we all got up to go Lewis grabbed me and kissed me again. I was worried about looking inexperienced, or slutty. It was hard to know how to act in front of his friends.

"Hey, meet me in the parking lot," he said, "and I'll drive you home."

The girls were watching me, disbelief written across their faces. I knew what they were thinking. What does he see in mousy Mia?

In the parking lot Lewis stood talking to Selena, a beautiful grade twelve girl. My guts shriveled as I saw their body language—they were totally into each other. Lewis was smiling and nodding at her and she was laughing. I clutched the strap on my bag tighter and stopped, watching him. I thought I might throw up. He saw me and waved me over. I tried to smile, but it felt like my face was making this really ugly twitching. I walked toward him with a phoney smile on my face.

"Selena, this is my girlfriend, Mia," he said, draping his arm over my shoulder.

My face twitched again and I held my hand over my cheek. He'd called me his girlfriend!

"Hi," she said, her eyes flicking briefly over me. "So, can I have a lift then?" She looked back at Lewis.

"Sure," he said. "You don't mind sitting in the back, do you?"

I shook my head and went to the back door while he opened the front passenger door.

"Mia?" he said, looking at me strangely.

"What?" I asked, my hand on the door handle.

"Aren't you getting in the front with me?"

"Yeah," I said, laughing suddenly, "of course. I was just putting my bag in."

Selena opened her own door and got in the back. I tried to hide my broad grin from both of them.

sophie

It took a lot of pleading to stop Dominic from trying to find Glenn and beating him up with a tire iron. He wanted to keep talking about that night too, but I couldn't say anything more. It was hard to keep it in perspective, to remember that Glenn was to blame, not me. But all I saw was *me* pressing that bus exit button, *me* walking through the streets holding his hand. I wouldn't talk about it anymore. Not with Dom, not with the police. I'd get through it somehow, like I got through the Westcroft crap.

"Don't push it," I finally snapped at Dom. "I'm not going to report it."

I knew he was only trying to help me, but all I wanted was to forget about it. I didn't want his sympathy.

And then there was Mia. It was beyond ironic—she wasn't a virgin anymore, and I was. She was so happy about being with Lewis Scott, but for me the whole situation was plain weird because now, in my mind, Lewis was as bad as Glenn. It was Lewis who'd driven off and left me with his *friend*.

I felt older than Mia and corrupted. She might've had sex, but she still seemed wide-eyed and impressed by Lewis and his crew. And as much as I didn't want to even say his name, I knew I had to warn her about Glenn.

After a couple of failed attempts I blurted out, "When I went to Glenn's place something awful happened."

"Yeah? What?" She smiled in a shared-knowledge way, like now she really understood what I meant.

"No, Mia, listen to me." I was sweating, unsure how to word it right. "Glenn gave me something."

"What?" She sat up, interested. "What was it?"

"I don't know. It wasn't good." I shook my head at her. She thought it was just another party drug. "He slipped something into my drink."

"Yeah? What happened?"

I tilted my head and scanned her face. The way she said it, her voice was laden with judgment. Like, "Oh, here we go, what's your excuse now?" I suddenly saw something I'd never seen before—she felt morally superior to me.

"I think …" and then I stopped. I looked at her looking at me and was overwhelmed by a sense of alienation. She didn't know me at all. And I didn't know her either.

"He's really rough," I said. "I think he's dangerous."

For a second her eyes narrowed with concern, but then she nudged me and pointed to my still-bruised lip. "Oh, do you mean he likes to play rough?"

"Mia, this isn't funny. I'm serious."

She nodded. "Okay, I get it."

She wasn't listening to me. "Promise me you'll stay away from him," I said finally.

"I said, I get it," she snapped and turned the subject back to Lewis. It sounded to me like she didn't get it at all. She acted like I was a parent telling her off. So I didn't say what I'd wanted to say.

In the week following that conversation things between us almost seemed back to normal. Lewis was away from school and Mia was desperate. I thought he was being a pig. Not one phone call or text.

"I thought he'd at least text," she said. She was trying not to cry.

"I know, he should have, but sometimes guys are just … different from us," I said, thinking about Thomas and Glenn. But then I reminded myself about Dominic. "Don't stress, he'll have a reason. Family emergency, an illness or something." *Or he's just a self-centered prick.* I smiled reassuringly at her.

"Oh God, Sophie," she said, taking my hand, "I think I've made a terrible mistake."

I shook my head, even though I agreed with her. But then I guess I was kind of relieved too. If Lewis never called her again she wouldn't call him, and then we'd move on. It would be like that weekend never happened. And even though she'd be devastated I knew she'd get over him.

Then Friday morning she messaged me before school. The message seemed to dare me.

Lewis texted
all ok—woz sic like u said
cum 2 party w me & L
B huge
plz

No way. No way no way no way. Lewis and a party. Glenn could easily be there too. I couldn't do it. I never wanted to see his face again as long as I lived. Mia would have to manage on her own.

mia

Everything was shiny and happy: shiny, happy people. I couldn't stop grinning. My life was perfect. Mom and I were getting on great, she was treating me with respect and finally allowing me to be an adult. I was full of love toward everyone in my life. I knew when I walked through the school grounds that people knew who I was now: Lewis Scott's girlfriend.

In class I'd get my work done quickly and then sit doodling, thinking about Lewis and the weekend just gone, or the weekend to come. Soph was still my best friend, even though we didn't hang out together so much anymore. She never wanted to come to any of the parties. She'd always come up with an excuse, and in the end I stopped asking.

In class she started hanging out with Adele, who is the biggest brainiac in our year. She knows the answer to everything and goes to the library at lunchtime to study. It's no great surprise that Adele aims to get into medicine or law. She'll probably be voted valedictorian next year. Most of us respect her, but she's not the sort of girl you'd want to hang out with. Or spend time with on the weekends. But now I watch Soph take her workbook over to Adele and see the way their heads almost touch as they go through the questions together. I reach for my iPod–one of my many presents from Lewis.

"What's this?" I asked, attempting nonchalance when he sat next to me on the bed and handed me the gift-wrapped box.

"A little present." He sat back and watched me unwrap it. There was no false Oh, you shouldn't have or any attempt on my part to give it back. Lewis wanted me to have nice things.

"Thanks," I said, leaning over and rewarding him with the only gift I had to offer.

Now in class I sit listening to the latest music Lewis has uploaded for me. I hear the other kids whisper about the stuff he gives me. I know it makes me sound like I'm full of myself but I feel so sophisticated. You would have thought I'd be jealous about Soph and Adele working together, but I'm not. It would be silly and childish. Life's too short to worry about who's doing what with whom. So I fall into the rhythm of the music and draw my little butterflies landing on apples surrounded by the initials LS, linking everything together.

Lewis was sitting in the cafeteria when I walked up at lunchtime. I leaned over to kiss him and noticed Sasha and Tanisha pass one of their looks. What? Sometimes these girls are so bitchy. But I wasn't going to let them spoil my day; I listened to Lewis and Ian talking about some tribal thing. I had no idea what they were going on about, but I nodded and smiled anyway.

"So," Lewis said finally, "do you want to come?"

"Where?" I asked.

"Two Tribes."

"Sure," I said, unsure about what I was agreeing to.

Two Tribes it turned out, was a huge dance festival. I'd never been to any type of music festival before, but apparently this was one of the best. Except it was an over-eighteen event.

"How'll I get in?" I asked Lewis casually, not wanting to look like I might be scared of getting busted for being underage. I'd never even gone to a nightclub before.

"I've got you a ticket already," he said.

"No, I meant ID."

"You'll be all right," he said confidently. "You're with me."

Two Tribes was on the long weekend. After school on Friday I stood waiting at Lewis's car with the bag of clothes I'd shoved in my locker that morning. Mom had been a bit hesitant about me staying over when she realized Lewis's parents were in China. But there really wasn't a lot she could do.

"Wouldn't you rather know where I was?" I demanded.

"Yes," she said, wiping furiously at the countertop, "but you're still fifteen. I don't think you're old enough to be alone at your boyfriend's."

I almost snorted. If she only knew. But I was learning to play my cards right with my mom.

"You know I'd never do anything stupid," I said, looking her in the eye. "And Lewis is really responsible."

She gave a small smile and nodded her head. "I know, but please be careful." She squeezed my hand. "You don't want to make the same mistakes I did."

I was so relieved that she'd given in, I didn't really give her comment a lot of thought.

We were sitting on Lewis's couch listening to The Kills and letting the first E kick in when the doorbell sounded. Lewis squeezed my leg as he got up. I smiled at him and shifted my gaze to the rolling surf beyond the picture window. If I could reach through the glass I'd almost be able to touch it. I felt the water running through the webbing of my fingers, tiny grains of sand fitting beneath my nails, the salt air in my mouth. I was smiling dreamily, as Lewis came back in with Glenn and a girl called Nicola.

"Hi," I said. "Are we going?"

"In a sec." Glenn sat down and pulled a bag out of his pocket and began making lines of white powder on the glass-topped coffee table. He chopped at it with his Visa card and winked at me. "Wanna line?"

Lewis picked up a straw and knelt in front of the table. I watched him snort one line, sniff loudly, and then snort another. He passed the straw to Glenn. "Coke," he said to me, twitching his lip and then rubbing his nose with the back of his hand.

I wasn't sure. I felt safe with Es. I'd talked to plenty of people who took them every weekend. But then everyone raved about coke, how fantastic it made you feel.

"It's a buzz," Lewis encouraged. "You'll love it."

I took the straw from Nicola, feeling excited and nervous. There were two lines left.

"Just do one," Lewis said, kneeling next to me. "A half each side."

I put the plastic straw in my nostril and sniffed, sliding it up the line as I went. The coke hit the inside of my nose with a powerful sting. I stopped and coughed. My nose was on fire. I sniffed heavily.

"Shit." I rubbed my knuckle over the end of my nose, almost regretting my decision.

"Take it slowly," Lewis coached.

I used the other nostril to snort the rest of the line, my nose burning unbearably. The dry, scorching rawness was too much and the back of my throat was also dry.

While Lewis and Glenn shared the last line I went into the kitchen for a drink. I was standing in front of the open fridge when suddenly the rush hit me. I was immediately euphoric, the fire in my nose gone. Holding on to the fridge handle, I stared into the shiny brightness of the gleaming shelves at rows of neatly stacked food. The colors of the labels were dazzling in their luminosity: peanut butter, Newman's Own Balsamic Vinaigrette, dill pickles, low-fat yogurt. The dark green skin of a cucumber glowed. The frothy green head of a bunch of baby carrots fizzed. I leaned into the side of the fridge and listened to it hum. The food sparkled, and the humming filled my body.

"Hey." Glenn was leaning against the island bench watching me.

I smiled securely. I'd never felt so fantastic before, not even on ecstasy. There was something so powerful about the cocaine, it made me lose the last scrap of self-doubt I had. I loved it.

"Looking forward to the concert?" I asked as I poured Glenn a drink.

His dark eyes watched me over his glass.

"I've never been to one before," I said, "I'm really excited."

"That right?" he said. I chatted away. I wasn't awkward or self-conscious. I was completely comfortable in my own skin, exhilarated.

"Ready?" Lewis came in. "We need to be there before lunch."

"Before DJ Samantha Ronson," I said firmly, though I had no idea who that was.

Security checked our cooler at the entrance to the gardens.

No alcohol or drugs were allowed, and all water bottles had to be sealed. One of the guys looked at me for such a long time that I was sure they were going to ask for ID. Lewis had his arm around me and I leaned in to his side, demonstrating my right to be there. Finally they let us through. I'd been holding my breath and quickly let it go. The high from the coke hadn't lasted long, and I was disappointed to feel it peeling away.

We went from one stage to another, leaving our cooler and blankets to mark our spot under the shade of a massive old oak tree. It was a fantastic day. The place was a crush of people. If this was early, I couldn't wait to see how many more turned up. It was going to be massive.

Lewis had a map and a timetable of the festival and he'd circled all the DJs he wanted to see. I leaned back against the grass, watching him sucking on the end of his red pen.

He looked over at me watching him. "What?"

"Nothing," I said, pleased with myself. When I stopped for a second, like this, it still amazed me to think of where I was and who I was with.

"Hey," Glenn said, opening a plastic bag, "who's up for a Mitsubishi?"

"Me," I said, straightening up and reaching over to pick a green pill out of his hand. I swallowed it quickly, the rush of taking pills out in public almost as thrilling as the pill itself.

Then DJ Ronson appeared on the stage. The roar from the crowd swelled through our bodies like a wave and the air was punctuated with blasting dance music. We sprang to our feet and joined the crowd pulsing to the beat of the music.

When you're rolling you know no time. It's like being suspended in space. Lewis was dancing with his eyes clamped tightly shut, and the beads of sweat rolling in tiny rivers down his neck made me realize how hot I was. I stopped and wiped a hand across my forehead. My hair was stuck to my face. I could feel my heart thundering in my chest. I glanced over at the cooler, standing alone, a blue-and-white beacon on a green checkered picnic blanket. Water. I imagined the bottles nestled among the cubes of ice, cold and wet.

I made my way to the cooler and pulled out a bottle and lifted it eagerly to my lips. But Lewis came up behind me and snatched it from my hand, slopping water all over me.

"Not that one," he said, quickly screwing the lid back on. "That's Glenn's."

I stared at him, surprised. He'd never been rough with me before.

Immediately he softened and gently took hold of my arm. "Sorry, Mia, this one's his. It's got a different lid, see?"

"What's the difference?" I asked, taking the bottle Lewis handed me instead and drinking it greedily.

"Glenn's laced this one and resealed it." He shook his head, watching Glenn, who was dancing energetically with Nicola. "GHB. Gutter shit. You don't want to do that." He tucked it back among the ice in the cooler.

I smiled at him and chugged my water, comforted by the way he looked after me. I didn't know what GHB was, but if Lewis thought it was bad, I didn't want any.

We were waiting for Goldfrapp to hit the stage. This had been one of the best days of my life.

Glenn pulled out his plastic bag. "Want one?" he said, shaking out the last handful of pills.

"Yeah." I picked out an E between my thumb and forefinger, but I didn't even have a chance to raise it to my lips before a security guard rushed through the crowd at us, his eyes fixed on the pills in Glenn's hand. I quickly shoved my hand in my pocket. So busted. The adrenaline whooshed upwards, making me feel light-headed and nauseous at the same time.

"Hey," the guard shouted, grabbing Glenn's arm. "What's that?"

"What?" Glenn flung the pills in a wide arc through the air and away from us. He straightened, hands on hips, and stared at the man.

My mouth was dry, my stomach freaking out.

"I saw you with drugs," the security guard shouted. Then, horribly, two more guards appeared around us. Instantly I thought of Mom, what she would say. I'd be so grounded. And that would only be the beginning. What if they brought the cops in? I tried to look calm as I shoved the pill deeper into my pocket. But they weren't looking at me, only at Glenn.

"I've got nothing," he said defiantly, showing his hands to the guard.

The first guard looked at the other two. Now I was anxiously wiping my hands down the front of my jeans. What now? What would they do? If they took us away and searched us I'd have to swallow the pill. Would they do a drug test? Shit, oh shit. They would surely call my mom.

The second guard shook his head at the first. I watched Glenn. His arms were crossed and he stared scornfully at them.

"What?" he sneered, shrugging his shoulders

contemptuously. "What are you going to do about it?"

"I'm watching you, buddy," the guard snarled, stalking off.

"Fucking loser," Glenn muttered, dropping to his hands and knees where the pills would've landed. I crouched down next to him, my heart thundering in my throat. I was so relieved we hadn't been taken away and questioned or searched.

Like a metal detector Glenn swept his hands over the grass. "Fuck. Two hundred bucks' worth." Then he grinned at me. "Got one."

I got on my hands and knees and helped him look. We found another, but that was all.

"Don't worry about it," he said, standing up.

I nodded, the fear completely gone. I looked around for the guards, mindful of the pill still in my pocket.

Glenn brazenly stuck his two on the end of his tongue. "They can't do anything. They can't prove a thing."

His confidence was reassuring. I pulled the pill out of my pocket and swallowed it too in a mix of relief and excitement at the narrowness of our escape.

sophie

It was a strange, disembodied stage that followed. One minute Mia and I were inseparable, then she was gone. Even though she still sat next to me, she had moved away from me, so happily and obliviously toward her dream. When we talked I saw the distance in her eyes. She listened and nodded, but she wasn't interested. She wasn't really there. It was the same if we chatted on MSN at night. Sometimes there'd be really long breaks between her replies because I was just one of many windows she had open. Her mind was always on Lewis Scott. He was all she ever spoke about: Lewis this, Lewis that. I grinned and nodded—and ground the enamel off my back teeth.

It hadn't taken long for Lewis Scott to monopolize every single conversation we had. Even if we were discussing something else, she'd steer the talk back to him. Sometimes I just wanted to slap her. "Listen to yourself," I wanted to scream. But in her current state of evolution she would have thought I was just envious. In the new order of Mia, that was her standard response. The days of steely sulks were replaced now with a dismissive "talk to the hand" gesture and her mantra "they're just jealous." She moved sublimely above everyone else, including me.

She didn't know about Dominic, that we were kind of back together. He was still my secret. Even if she'd given me the chance, if she'd ever stopped for breath, I wouldn't have wanted to share that news with her. She wouldn't have understood. Worse, I thought she wouldn't really care.

She had this superior attitude to everything now, like she thought she was married and the rest of us were immature kids pretending to be grown up. It was an attitude that came through in her new smile, and her willingness to pass judgment on almost everyone and everything. If Mia wanted to be the Most Hated Girl in School, she was chalking up the points quickly. My smart, funny friend had turned into a shallow, self-absorbed, boring pain in the ass.

But call me optimistic. I thought, one day Lewis Scott is going to move on to someone else, and when he dumps her, we'll have the old Mia back.

So we were engaged in this farce. Still pretending we were best friends, sitting together in class, sharing notes and textbooks, but come the end of the day, I walked away from her with relief. I'd leave her to swagger to the student parking lot where she'd lean against Lewis's car, chatting to all the grade twelves, waiting for him to drive her home.

And I didn't know what was happening between Dom and me anyway. He'd text me every morning, some small message, like: how u doin? C U @ skool

And I'd reply with some standard response to say I was okay, but it was a lie. I was not okay, and he knew it. He was still offering me help, support, and comfort, but I didn't want it. I wanted him to want me like before, when he saw me as a whole person, strong and invincible, not some victim in need of rescuing. While I responded to his texts, I still couldn't bring myself to be totally truthful with him and so I mostly avoided him at school. And Mia's popular grade twelves—I used any excuse not to join them, they were far too nauseating.

I knew I shouldn't be cutting myself off. In fact I felt really confused—and the loneliest I had ever been. I still wasn't all right about what happened that night with

Glenn, and I sort of knew I needed help to get over it. But the help I needed didn't exist, or at least that's what I thought. So I kept my mouth shut, went to the library and studied, and remembered a time when I had someone I could have told all this to.

mia

After a big weekend I always found Tuesdays harder than Mondays. By Tuesday I'd bottomed out, which left me feeling empty and flat. Nothing would lift me up, not even thinking about Lewis. It was easy to see everything negatively. I wanted to touch and feel thrilled, but instead I felt empty and lonely, isolated from everyone as if there was a barrier around me that nothing could penetrate. I hated it.

"Hi, Jordie," I said, leaning in the doorway of his room and watching my brother glue parts to his model airplane. He glanced up at me quickly, tongue sticking out slightly, then went back to his plane.

"Whatchya doing?" I asked, though it was obvious. I slumped on the end of his bed.

He had both hands tightly clamping a wing to his B-52. I knew it was a B-52 because the instructions–or destructions, as Jordie used to say–were spread out in front of him like a tourist map. I looked at the back of his head, bowed over in concentration, and I felt an overwhelming urge to touch him, like he was a little baby again, and I used to stroke the side of his face to help him go to sleep. The compulsion was so strong it surprised me.

"I think it's off," he mumbled.

"What?" I asked, startled by the sound of his voice.

"The glue," he said, releasing the wing, which promptly fell off the body of the plane. "Damn," he said sharply.

"Can I help?" I leaned down and picked the wing up, looking for a reason to stay in his room. "If I hold it for longer it might stick. You can build another bit."

He gave me a funny look but re-glued the wing and stuck it back in position, then gingerly passed it to me. I held the wing against the engine air intake.

"It's a long-range bomber," he said, holding up a brush tipped with green paint, "originally designed to carry nuclear weapons."

"Really?"

"Yeah." He applied quick brushstrokes to the tip of the plane's tail. "I'm gonna be a pilot. But not a bomber one."

"Really?" I said again, but this time the surprise showed in my tone.

"Mia," Jordie frowned, "I've always wanted to be a pilot, since forever."

I nodded as if I remembered, but actually I had no idea. I carried out my task carefully, making sure the wing was in the exact position Jordie had placed it in. The truth was, I knew very little about Jordie. There was a time I'd known him really well, in the months after Dad left. The two of us had stuck together. Sitting in his room reminded me of how I'd actually enjoyed his company, when we used to talk and he'd make me laugh. Suddenly I was overwhelmed with nostalgia. I suppressed the urge to cry and focused on my little brother's animated face telling me the history of the B-52.

"Do you know one of its nicknames was BUFF?"

I shook my head. "Why?"

"It stands for Big Ugly Fat" –he dropped his voice and leaned closer, eyes glinting delightedly– "Fuckers!"

"Jordie!" We both laughed, watching the doorway for Mom.

"It's stuck," I said finally, holding my part of the plane aloft for his approval.

"Cool," he said, taking it from my hands. "Thanks."

I watched him lay the pieces side by side. So neat and precise. He'd finished building for today. Reluctantly I got up off the bed.

"Wanna play Xbox?"

"Sure," I said gratefully, "but I warn you, I will be kicking your butt."

With my new status at school came new responsibility. I had to look good all the time. I couldn't have other girls eyeing me, wondering what Lewis Scott saw in that pimply scrag. I watched what I ate, though I wasn't in danger of getting fat. Most weekends I ate nothing anyway, and all the dancing was burning up heaps of calories. But it didn't look good to sit around eating crap in front of everyone. Most of the time we ate nothing and drank diet soft drinks.

"So what color is it?" Sasha asked, holding a few strands of Tanisha's hair up to the sunlight.

"Chestnut."

I filled them in on the latest hair fashion, which was a weave of three different tones. I knew my stuff. I studied *Cosmo* like some people study the Bible. I knew every trend and fashion statement.

"I'm getting mine done this weekend," I said.

"Cool," Sasha said.

I'd had a major fight with Mom, but I'd made the appointment anyway.

"I don't know why you have to be like everyone else," she'd said, shaking her head at me.

"I'm not, it's about looking good and fashionable."

"Fashion is another word for conformity," she said.

"Looking at all the gray in your hair, you might want to conform a little," I snapped.

She wouldn't get off my back, even about something as stupid as hair color. So what if I put a few highlights in my hair. Lewis's birthday was next week and there was no way I was helping host his party with drab, mousy hair.

I stopped to use the bathroom on my way to English class. I was busting, but I was so late anyway that a few more minutes wouldn't make any difference. I heard someone come in. Two people. My ears honed in on my name, uttered with pure venom.

"Mia." It was dragged out nastily, petulantly. Meeeee-a.

The other girl laughed, just as meanly. "She's such a skank."

Tanisha and Sasha.

"I know." There was the sound of a tap running. "She's so full of herself. Does she really think we give a shit about her opinion?"

"Oh, I know." Tanisha mimicked my voice: "This season's all about chestnut!"

They laughed together.

"What a slut."

"How long, do you figure?"

"Dunno. He's had his cherry now. Couple more weeks?"

"If that."

"Well, you know Lewis. Nice and young, a bit of fun, then see ya later."

"Yeah, but usually they're better looking. I mean he's such a hottie. He must know he can do better than Miss Thing."

"Sash, don't stress. It won't take him long to figure it out. Don't worry. You'll have him for the prom."

"I guess."

The door opened, then shut again. The toilet in the next cubicle hissed quietly, then there was silence. My cheeks were hot. I knew there was no one out there, but I was cautious anyway leaving the cubicle. Pair of bitches. They're just jealous, I told my reflection. Sasha wants him. For the prom? I shook my head. I don't think so.

sophie

Dom was picked for an exhibition game and was flying across the country. He was going to be gone for two weeks and that made me aware of just how important it was for me to know he was around.

He had started calling me at night when I wouldn't see him at school. Just listening to his voice made me feel connected to the world again. He didn't talk about that night anymore, or about Mia or any of that scene. He just talked to me about whatever.

One night he started talking about his dad. To Dom, he is a real hero. He had closed his medical practice to work with people living with AIDS and HIV, mostly in the Sudan. But he doesn't broadcast his deeds, expecting to be admired. He does what is in his heart, what makes a difference to him.

"I'll call you as often as I can," Dominic said, "but it probably won't be every night."

"That's okay." I tried to laugh. "Go and win."

The buzz at school had been Lewis Scott's birthday party. I watched people approach Mia and ask her some detail—probably about what pills would be there—and she'd smile in that patronizing way she'd cultivated. I didn't ask her one single thing about it. I couldn't bring myself to have that worldly gaze of hers bestowed upon me. And frankly, I didn't give a shit about the party. I'd rather sit at home and pluck my bikini line with a pair of tweezers than go to their Pill Popping Party.

I couldn't imagine ever relaxing and having fun at a party again. I had a real fear of alcohol—scared that if I had a drink I might lose control, or that it might be spiked. I was scared of pills too. I'm not a stupid person. Straight, I wouldn't get into a car with someone I don't know, so why did I get off the bus that night when I knew I wanted to stay on it? That wasn't how I want to live my life, scared of stuff.

I watched Mia's transformation into this new person and it was easy to blame the pills. Who really knew what was in them? When she stuck those pills in her mouth I know she wasn't thinking that they might have Drano in them, or battery acid. She refused to look at any of the negative stuff because nothing negative had happened to her. Everything she'd always wanted had fallen in her lap—a good-looking, rich boyfriend and a full-on social life. It was just about the feel-good time she was going to have. But she changed so much. The pills made her selfish and inconsiderate. She never used to be like that.

mia

Lewis's party was going to be the event of the year. We spent most lunchtimes discussing invites, drinks, music, drugs. Lewis wasn't sparing any expense. People would ask me about it because I was his girlfriend. It made me feel really good, knowing people respected me, but sometimes, on a Tuesday or Wednesday, when I was always a bit flat, I'd feel like no one came up to me because of me, Mia, but only because I was Lewis's girlfriend. On those days, though, everything was a drag, especially school, which was starting to slip. I kept promising myself that I'd have a weekend off and catch up, but every weekend there was something on, and I couldn't bear to miss out. Sometimes at Dad's I'd get some work done, but mostly Jordie went to Dad's alone. Who knew what I might miss if I skipped a party?

Even though the other girls seemed to be my friends and talked to me at parties, I just couldn't forget what

Tanisha and Sasha had been discussing in the bathroom. Lewis's party would be our three-month anniversary. What if he dumped me? Sasha wouldn't be the only one ready to move in on him. The idea of losing him made me crazy.

And even if it was because they were jealous, knowing what those two really thought of me made me feel horribly alone. Who knows what anyone else truly feels when they're laughing and smiling with you? Soph would've known, but even though we still sat next to each other in class, I didn't really have her anymore.

It made me feel really sad thinking about the good times we used to have, even here at school. Suddenly I remembered the incident with Mr. Lush and I laughed out loud. I glanced around the classroom quickly, but everyone was busy working, so I pushed my earpiece in deeper and drew butterflies on my page. Mr. Lush was a student teacher we'd had back in grade ten. He was one of the most appropriately named people in the world—totally luscious, with a body to die for. His major area was of course phys ed. School had never been so good.

At lunchtime on Mr. Lush's last day, Soph and I were in the art room, rushing to complete my screen print project. We'd managed to get it nearly finished, but then we saw we were both late for class, so we rushed off.

As I ran up a flight of stairs ahead of Soph, I noticed I hadn't cleaned my hands. They were still covered in wet paint. Just in front of us, moving at a snail's pace, was William McRobbin, a guy in our grade who we'd known since forever. William was on the football team, and was totally well built.

"Hey, Billy boy," I shouted, slapping his bum through his white football pants. "Hustle your ass."

He turned–and of course it wasn't William but Mr. Lush.

I nearly died. Soph was on the stairs right behind me. In my horror I took an involuntary step backward and slipped down the stairs onto Soph. Mr. Lush tried to grab me but down I went, taking Soph with me. We became a human snowball, rolling down the steps until we reached the landing. Luckily, only our dignity was hurt. Well, destroyed. I was mortified. I thought, Thank God he's leaving. It was totally embarrassing.

Mr. Lush ran down the stairs to check us for damage, but couldn't get anything intelligible out of either of us. All we could do was lie there laughing. Once he had helped us up and gone ahead to his class, we laughed all the louder. On his bum, where I'd slapped him, was a bright-red handprint.

But now Soph had drifted away, just because I had a

boyfriend. I had never let go of our friendship all the times she had a guy. I couldn't believe how she'd just abandoned me. I'd given up asking her to come out with us–there are only so many rejections a person can take. She didn't like what I was up to, and because she'd become so anti-drugs, I didn't tell her. Anyway, what she was doing I found totally boring, living in the library with other grade eleven wannabes. But remembering how things used to be made me really want her to come to Lewis's party.

"It'll be great, Soph," I pleaded. It surprised me how much I wanted her to say yes. I hated the awkwardness that had grown between us. "It's gonna be huge. Please say you'll come."

"I don't know." She looked at me dubiously. "It's not really my scene. Won't everyone be wasted?"

There was something so judgmental in the way she said it. Like we were all a bunch of losers.

"Soph! We don't do drugs all the time."

She raised her eyebrow and sighed.

"Please, Soph, it'll be like old times." As I said it, I really hoped that it would be.

She was silent for a long while and I didn't think she was even going to answer. "Sorry," she said finally. "Yeah, I'll come. What're you going to wear?"

Lewis and I set up the kegs and the bottles of water, and I put floating candles and flowers in the pool. Then we both dropped a couple of Es.

I swallowed them quickly. It hadn't taken long for one pill to not be enough–we could take up to four in a night. To bring us down we had to smoke more weed, but it was all good.

By the time guests started arriving I was totally up. This was like my home now, and I showed people where to put their bags and got drinks for them. Lewis was ecstatic, literally. He was laughing and smiling, and I knew, as I looked at him across the room, this was going to be a night I'd never forget.

I saw Soph arrive, hovering near the door clutching her bag. I swooped on her immediately. "Come in, come in," I said, leading her to Lewis's bedroom. "Pretty amazing, hey?"

"Yeah." She dropped her bag on the bed. "Mia, have you–"

I cut her short. Now wasn't the time for a lecture. "Yeah, I was a bit nervous. Do you want one?"

She shook her head. "Nah, I think I'll stick with vodka."

sophie

Adele is a majorly smart girl. I'd always been a bit intimidated by her. She looked like some boring study geek with no social life, but when I got to know her I saw she was a lot more than that. True, her priority is doing well at school, above all else, but I have to admire her determination. She knows what she wants and isn't going to let anything stand in her way. And she has fun too, once the studying is done.

Adele was having a party on the same night as Lewis Scott. Not that there would be any conflict for anyone about which party to go to, because the two groups were socially miles apart.

I was kind of excited about Adele's party. It was an opportunity to test myself, to see if I could still have a social life and not be so terrified all the time. And that was something I really wanted. I was getting sick of the isolation. Dom's absence, after just one day, had made me painfully aware of that. And I figured if Adele and Dom were capable of juggling everything, so was I.

It seemed like Mia really wanted me at Lewis's, and not just to show off as Miss Popularity. I didn't want to tell her I was going to a different party. That would've been like acknowledging our friendship was over. I couldn't bring myself to admit that yet. I didn't want to tell her how different we were now, how we had nothing in common anymore. Part of me still hoped that when she broke up with Lewis I'd be there for her and she'd go back to her old self.

When she suggested it could be like old times I realized she missed me too and wanted our old friendship back, so I agreed to go. I certainly wasn't imagining everything would suddenly be fixed between us, but it could be a start, a reminder to both of us that what we had was too important to forget. I figured I could just stay for an hour, then slip away to Adele's.

The party was everything I thought it would be—totally pumping from the minute I walked up the footpath. Lewis's parents were rolling in cash, and there was something grotesque about the display of wealth. I felt uncomfortable before I even walked in the front door, and the feeling worsened the minute Mia greeted me. I guess she toned it down a bit at school, because that night I saw the new Mia in full force. I saw in her face how proud she was of what she thought she'd become. She acted like she owned the place and it made me feel sick.

I had a drink to take my mind off it all. And then I had another one and another after that, and I guess that's what did it. It was the first time I'd drunk anything since that night at Glenn's. I was starting to relax and having a good time. I *wanted* to have a good time. There were people I knew, and the house was rocking. I made a decision to stay for as long as I was having fun.

mia

By ten the drinkers were trashed and the pillers rolling along nicely. I escaped to Lewis's room to use his bathroom. The ones downstairs had lineups, and why should I have to wait with the rest of them? I pushed open the bathroom door and saw Lewis standing in front of the basin. He turned around, startled.

"Hey, Mia, I was just coming to look for you."

"What're you doing?" I asked, eyeing the lines on the vanity top.

"I got some coke," he said, nodding toward it. "I promised Sasha she could have some."

I looked past him at Sasha perched on the edge of the toilet seat and my guts tripped out. I didn't know what to say. It felt like something was going on, like I'd just busted them, but I didn't want to say anything and see it all blow up in my face. Lewis's head was down, his blond fringe flapping forward as he snorted the line.

161

"Here, babe," he said as he handed me the rolled fifty, but he was looking at Sasha, not me, and frowning slightly.

Now I looked at her, trying to smile, and she gave me a fake smile in return.

I snorted the remaining two lines. "Oh," I said, like I'd just remembered, "sorry, did you want some too?"

Sasha left the bathroom and I made out with Lewis. It seemed really important to get him hot for me. After about fifteen minutes I pulled away and straightened my hair.

"We'd better go back," I murmured.

"In a minute," he said, grabbing me around the waist.

Back downstairs the party was even wilder. I let go of Lewis's hand and watched him walk toward a group of friends. I felt supremely confident again. I saw Sasha sitting in a corner with Tanisha and smiled to myself. Stupid bitch, trying to compete with me. I got a drink and walked through to the games room. Some guys were playing pool, and I saw Sophie leaning against the bar. I'd hardly seen her since she got here.

She was talking to Glenn. After our near-drug bust at Two Tribes, he and I seemed to share a bit of a bond. But he was into much harder stuff than Lewis and me, and sometimes he made me nervous, especially when I'd smoked weed—it can do that to me, make me a little paranoid.

As I got closer, Soph began shouting at him. She sounded really drunk. Glenn shrugged, then shook his head at her. I thought she was going to hit him in the face. He put his hand out to touch her, but she pushed it away really violently. When I reached her she was crying and mascara was running down her cheeks.

"Soph, Soph, what's the matter? Chill out, Soph," I said, trying to bring her down.

"That guy is a fucking rapist," she spat, pointing at Glenn and swaying wildly. "He can't get chicks unless he drugs them and gangbangs them with his fucking friends …"

Exactly at the moment when I was thinking how pissed people never realize how drunk and stupid they sound, I was distracted from Sophie's incredible accusations by Tower. In fact I couldn't see Sophie anymore because things suddenly went mental. Tower lurched into the middle of the room, knocking into people and making this wild gurgling noise. He was foaming at the mouth and his eyes were rolling in his head.

People started to move back. Tower stood alone in the middle of the room, shuddering as the foam spilled out of his mouth.

Someone shouted, "Good one, Tower!" and then everyone started laughing with relief. Typical Tower, the practical joker. Foam sprayed from his mouth as he continued to jerk, and people kept laughing–until he crashed into a coffee table and dropped to the floor with a ground-shaking thud. Tiny shards of glass surrounded him like teardrops. And then he started to convulse. This was not a joke. I was frozen in horror. It was the most terrifying thing I'd ever seen.

I ran over and crouched down next to him. He was a mass of jerking, twitching limbs, and his body spasmed in ways I'd never have thought physically possible. His eyes were open and fixed on the ceiling as the foam spluttered from his mouth. It's an image I can't shake–those shiny whites of his eyes. He kept jerking, almost to the beat of the music. The laughter had stopped. Everyone was paralyzed with fear.

"Quick!" I screamed, suddenly finding my voice. "Call 911! Someone call a fucking ambulance."

Glenn grabbed hold of my arm, hard. "Don't be so hysterical," he warned.

Somebody was trying to restrain Tower and clear his airway. The convulsing stopped.

Roger, a friend of Lewis's, came running up with car keys jangling in his hand. "Get him into my car. We'll take him to Emergency."

Lewis had him under the arms and Roger had his feet.

The music still pounded, yet it suddenly seemed deathly quiet in the house. I watched them carry Tower through the doorway, foam still sputtering from his mouth, and ran after them to the car.

Roger raced us through the streets, driving wildly, darting in and out of traffic. I was turned in my seat watching Lewis cradling Tower's head in his lap as he sporadically twitched. Every now and then Lewis shook him hard. "Wake up, buddy," he shouted. "Wake up."

I stayed in the car in the ambulance bay as Roger and Lewis carried Tower into the emergency room. I was one hundred percent sober now. I kept seeing Tower hit the floor and convulse. I was terrified he would die. And as the moments dragged by I knew everything would be exposed now. The cops would be called in. My parents would find out. I shook and shook. I couldn't stop.

I was just opening the car door to go inside and see what was happening when Lewis and Roger came running back to the car. They jumped in and were still pulling their doors shut as Roger took off with squealing tires.

I looked at them in amazement. "That was quick. What did they say?"

Roger was driving as fast as he had on the way to the hospital. My fingers clutched the door handle tightly.

Neither of them would look at me.

"You told them what he'd taken? They need to know." I looked from one to the other. Neither one of them said a thing.

"Say something," I screamed. I was freaking out. Their silence was terrible. "Lewis, did you speak to anyone?"

He shook his head. "We don't know what he took, Mia. It could've been a combination of anything. If we'd hung around we all could've got into serious shit."

I couldn't believe what he was saying. "Roger?"

He took his eyes off the road for a second and glanced at me. "Lewis is right. They'll know what to do."

I shut my eyes. What had they done? "I can't believe you guys. He's your friend," I screamed at Lewis, my eyes filling with tears.

Finally he looked at me, stony-faced. "Fuck, Mia, if you're going to party like an adult you're going to need to grow up."

sophie

It was all over that night. There was no friendship left between Mia and me. What she did to me, you don't do to your friends. I felt abandoned and discarded and totally betrayed. I'd risked so much to go to that party for the sake of our friendship, but she didn't care about me at all. I was nowhere near as important as her drugged-out loser friends.

I knew when I agreed to go that Glenn would probably be there. I figured one day I was bound to bump into him and at least this way I could be prepared. Glenn was a covert operator. I, on the other hand, am not. No way was I going to ever again accept a drink from someone I didn't know and trust. I wasn't frightened of what he could do to me, it was the thought of seeing him at all that freaked me.

But when I did see him, leaning against the wall, I wasn't scared. Not one tiny bit. I was mad. I was really mad. I'd had a few drinks, and that probably gave me a strength I might not otherwise have had. He was so sleazy, so smug, it enraged me even more.

"Hey, Sophie Spencer." He eyed me up and down. "Long time no see."

"Funny about that," I said through gritted teeth. "You're lucky you're still around."

And then he touched me. His heavy, disgusting hand touched my arm and immediately jolted me into a state of panic.

"Don't you dare touch me." I hit his hand away really hard. "You fucking disgusting pig."

And then he laughed, that same amused giggle he'd made when I'd run terrified into his screen door.

"Relax, Sophie, it was only a bit of fun. You know how much you wanted it."

If Mia hadn't appeared just then I would've punched him in the face.

She was trying to calm me down, and I guess I must've looked pretty crazy. And then all of a sudden I knew what to do. Tell the truth. Right now. It seemed so obvious. Once she knew, that old Mia, hidden deep inside Miss Plastic Fantastic, would quickly rise up to support me.

But even as I began I faltered. Immediately her eyes

were filled with that same look I'd seen before when I'd tried to have this conversation. A look of judgment and disbelief. The patronizing look of someone who wishes you would accept responsibility for your own mess.

How had things got so bad? We weren't bad people. But Mia had turned into a total stranger. What she did and thought wasn't on any wavelength I occupied. It was ironic that she should think I had no control over my actions—that I was some cheap slut who did it with anyone, anytime. In spite of her skeptical face, I continued. She had to know what had happened.

But as I tried to explain how Glenn spiked drinks and assaulted girls, some party-hard giant staggered into the room with foam spilling out of his mouth. It was disgusting, and everyone was laughing. I thought, Who are you people? How is this funny? And Mia laughed along with them. She didn't want to know that I'd nearly been raped, that a friend of her boyfriend's had drugged me. She didn't care how I felt. She turned her back on me to join in with the joke.

I left then. I didn't need it spelled out any clearer than that. I knew, without a doubt, that it was over between us. For good.

mia

The house was empty when we got back. The lights were on, the music was still pumping, and the front door was wide open. I walked up the path behind Lewis, remembering the first time I'd entered his house. Inside, my heels clattered on the cold white tiles. Lewis turned the music down and I stood in the middle of the living room, arms wrapped tightly around myself, not knowing what to do. There were half-empty drinks and bottles all over the place. Glass crunched under my feet, and I automatically started to straighten the room.

"Leave it," Lewis said. "I've got the cleaners coming tomorrow."

I couldn't look at him. Suddenly his voice made me sick. Of course Lewis wouldn't clean up this mess. He'd get someone else to do it. I held back my tears.

"Here," he said, more softly. I looked at the pill in the palm of his hand and then I stared into his face. He looked like a little boy who'd been caught doing the wrong thing. He almost seemed surprised when I shook my head. "Thought it'd lighten the mood," he said, shrugging his shoulders.

He disgusted me. "You should have spoken to someone," I muttered, willing myself not to cry.

"That's what they're trained for, Mia. It's their job to figure it out."

I couldn't believe him and his friends. Everyone had abandoned Tower. Dump him and run, save yourself. Nothing was what I thought it was. I wiped away the tears that were sliding down my face.

Lewis stood coldly watching. "He'll be all right. Don't be such a fucking drama queen."

Tears blurred my vision as I looked for my bag. I didn't even know who he was. I watched him walk out to the backyard, then I opened the front door and let myself out.

At home I sat in my bedroom in the dark and cried and cried. I felt deluded and deceived and I had no idea how I'd ended up at this point. This was the scariest thing I'd ever experienced and no one could fix it. I thought of Tower alone in the hospital and prayed someone had called his parents. I hated the idea of him being there on his own. I willed him to be all right. I lay on my bed feeling empty and hollow, thinking about how seriously wrong everything had gone, and I cried over Lewis because he wasn't the person I thought he was.

I thought about Sophie too, and what she'd said about Glenn. I pulled the covers up to my chin and hugged my knees through the sheets. I couldn't believe that Glenn had raped her. Maybe she had done it with him, but then regretted it. After all, she hadn't told me, or gone to the police. But I'd never known Soph to lie before. I was so confused, I couldn't figure it out, and I knew I'd never sleep. Everything was so seriously wrong.

In the morning I stayed in my bedroom, still crying. When I left Lewis's all I'd wanted was to get the hell away from him. But now? I didn't want to split up. Outside my window it was a bright sunny morning, and it seemed to me now that Lewis had done the best he could. He'd only been protecting everyone. I should've stayed with him. I needed to call him. I was terrified I'd blown the best thing in my life. I picked up the phone when suddenly it rang loudly. I jumped and almost dropped it.

"Mia?" It was Lewis and he sounded awful.

"Hey." I breathed a huge sigh of relief. "I'm so sorry about last night."

He was silent. I listened to his breathing and felt myself panicking. This was it. He was breaking up with me.

"Lewis," I said loudly, "is everything all right? Can we talk?"

I heard his breath again and then a small noise.

"Lewis?" I whispered. I didn't want to speak. And I didn't want him to tell me it was over. I held my breath.

He cleared his throat. "He died, Mia."

I squeezed my eyes tightly shut. My breath jagged in my throat. I tried not to cry out.

"He had a massive heart attack. I just spoke to his dad. Will you come over?"

I stood under the hot spray and sobbed. Tower was dead. I turned off the taps and sat on the edge of the bath.

Tower had died.

I looked at myself in the mirror. I was scared.

Slowly I toweled myself dry and got dressed. I'd told Lewis I'd come, but now I didn't want to. I didn't want to see him. Maybe Tower would still be alive if Lewis had told

173

them everything we knew he'd taken. Maybe nothing would've made any difference. But it didn't really matter. Tower was dead.

"You okay?" Mom asked, her voice full of concern. "You look terrible."

I shook my head, not sure whether I could speak.

"Did something happen?" she asked, sitting next to me.

"Lewis and I split up," I said finally, allowing more tears to spill down my face.

"Oh sweetie." Mom grabbed my hand. "Why?"

I shook my head, like I didn't really know.

That weekend was the worst of my life. Mom left me alone, believing my tears were due to my break-up with Lewis. There was no way I was telling her about Tower. I lay on my bed listening to music—real music with lyrics, about love and betrayal and break-ups. I didn't think it was possible to cry as much as I did. Lewis called my house when I didn't turn up, but I shook my head at Mom.

"I don't want to talk to him," I said, waving her away.

I couldn't be near him and I couldn't listen to his voice. I know he hadn't thought Tower would die, but I couldn't believe how cowardly he was. I'd thought he was a god. He was none of the things I'd believed. He hadn't even tried to save his best friend's life. I was convinced that if only he and Roger had stayed and told the doctors what Tower had taken, he would have survived. And I blamed myself for just sitting in the car, waiting. I'd done nothing either.

On Monday morning I seriously considered skipping school. I didn't want to run into Lewis or any of his friends. And I was nervous about seeing Sophie. She'd know what had happened. Everyone would.

I avoided the cafeteria, walking halfway around the school so as not to go near it. People kept looking my way, but I turned my iPod up and ignored them all. I saw Sophie outside class.

"Soph," I called, running to catch up to her.

She stopped and turned. "What?"

"Sophie," I said, reaching over to touch her arm, "I'm sorry about Saturday night."

But she looked at me meanly. "Just forget it," she spat and turned her back.

I grabbed hold of her arm. "Soph, what happened with Glenn? Please talk to me. You can trust me, honestly."

She narrowed her eyes and glared at me. "You didn't want to know when I tried to tell you. Don't try to pretend you care now."

She couldn't be serious. She'd seen what had happened.

"But, Sophie," I pleaded, "Tower was overdosing."

"I guess that's the risk some people take," she said coldly. "Go and talk to your new friends, Mia. I'm not interested in anything you have to say."

And then she went to the other side of the room and sat next to someone else. I stood in the doorway in a state of shock. What the hell was the matter with her? How could she be so heartless? A person had died, for Christ's sake.

I sat on my own at the back of the class, pushed my ear bud in, and turned the music up. I noticed people looking my way, but I pretended to ignore them. After everything we'd been through, Sophie's betrayal was ultimate. And then it occurred to me maybe she didn't know that Tower had died. Maybe when she knew that, she'd soften.

At lunchtime I went to our bench, but Soph didn't show up. Outside it was a beautiful sunny day, but I felt cold. Through the open window I listened to the shrieks and shouts of people having fun on the diamond, the crack of a baseball, and I had no idea what to do with myself.

sophie

I made a decision that weekend, tucked into my bed, a crumpled pile of tissues in my lap and my photo albums spread out in front of me. I had to accept the changes. Mia had moved on, somewhere I didn't want to go. We had nothing—nada, zip, zero—in common anymore. In fact, I probably had more in common with Adele. Not her overwhelming passion for study, but her determination. I was resolved to like myself. I guess the biggest thing I got out of that night was this: Sophie Spencer deserves better. Sophie Spencer wants to be with people who like her for who she really is, who do not judge her for the mistakes she made.

So when Mia offered me an olive branch it was all I could do not to whack her with it, hard. "You can trust me," she said. Trust! She wouldn't have known trust if it bit her in the ass. No doubt she was wrecked over her break-up with Lewis, the talk of the school that morning in homeroom. But I wasn't going to be there to pick up the pieces. She would have to handle it on her own.

I was horrified to learn later that the guy at the party had died. There were plenty of rumors about the OD, though no one from school really knew him. But I did hear that Mia and Lewis just dumped him at the hospital and left him to die. By then, I didn't think she could do anything more to shock me, but I was disgusted that she could be so callous.

It seemed unbelievable. What Mia and her friends were up to was more than stupid, it was dangerous; it was killing people. For that reason too I couldn't be a part of her life anymore. It's called self-preservation—I learned about it in biology. In order to save yourself, you have to remove yourself from danger. And that's what I did.

I decided I couldn't afford to care about her anymore. She thought she was so tough and mature and adult she could handle anything that happened. Well, if she wanted to hang out with rapists and druggies, then let her. That was her attitude—you get what you deserve. I wouldn't talk to her and I couldn't look at her.

I was so glad when Dominic got back from his exhibition game.

mia

I couldn't go to Tower's funeral. I didn't think I'd be able to handle it. The foam, the whites of his eyes–I couldn't bear to remember them. I didn't want to look at Lewis and Roger as Tower was lowered into the ground. I read the report of his death in the paper. It was being treated as an accidental overdose. Inquiries into how he'd got to the hospital, or where he'd been before, were inconclusive. Lewis and Roger got what they wanted–no trouble on their heads. The toxicology report showed cocaine, alcohol, MDMA, LSD– and even rat poison. Why the hell was that there?

If I passed through the cafeteria, I'd dart a sideways glance toward Lewis and his group. But they were oblivious to me. I was Invisible Mia again, drifting through the school unseen and unheard. It was no great shock to see him and Sasha together. I'd heard the rumors–passed on with a bitchy smile by girls who had hated me being with Lewis– that they'd hooked up the day after the party.

I missed Soph so much. I tried to patch things up with her, but she completely cut me out. I texted and e-mailed her, trying to explain, but I don't know if she even read them. I tried talking to her at school, but she'd just get up and move away from me, or look straight through me like I was vapor. She was hanging out with mega-straight girls, and when they saw me coming they'd close in around her like they were protecting her from me. I realized then she thought I was scum.

At home things were just as bad. My Tuesday blues extended to every day now. Each morning when I woke it was with heaviness and dread. I could barely stand myself. I had nothing to offer anybody. Why would anyone want to be my friend? I was totally boring and uninteresting. I was constantly on the verge of tears. I spent hours locked in my room listening to music and staring at the wall or, worse, at my face in the mirror. I despised what I saw. A plain girl, with bland hair. I'd sneer at her and snarl. But she never fought back. I hated her.

One day Mom put her head around my door.

"What're you doing, honey?"

I shook my head.

She stepped into my room and sat on the edge of my bed. "You know, there'll be others …" she said.

I nodded but didn't want to speak. I missed Lewis and the life I'd been leading. I really missed the expensive gifts, the partying and excitement. And God, I missed the Es and the way they made me feel. I wanted to be that other Mia, that fashionable and fun one, the girl with a life. But also, I couldn't stop thinking about Tower, remembering the whites of his eyes.

"You've got to go out and do things," Mom said, standing up. "Why don't you call Sophie and have a girls' night. We never see her anymore."

"Maybe," I said. But I wouldn't call Sophie because she'd just hang up on me.

sophie

"Soph?"

Dominic's voice startled me. It was easy to drift off in companionable silence with him. I was the most comfortable I'd ever been in my own skin with Dom around. It hadn't taken long for Dom to become a natural part of my life. There was no pressure from him. He seemed to just like being with me. The relief at giving up the old act was indescribable.

"What?" I said, sitting up.

"It's not your birthday yet, but I can't wait any longer." He was smiling widely. "Can I give it to you now?"

He handed me a small square box, which could only mean one thing. A ring.

"Oh, Dom," I said anxiously, but he just laughed.

"Open it, Soph. Don't be scared, it's not an engagement ring, I promise."

I lifted the lid. Inside, nestled in the black velvet padding, sparkled a diamond friendship ring. I pulled it out of the box.

"Oh, Dom," I said again, open-mouthed and almost speechless.

He laughed, delighted with my reaction. "Does it fit?"

I slid it onto my ring finger and it fit perfectly. It was so pretty. I loved it. "Thank you," I said, holding my hand out to admire it. "It's beautiful."

"Good," he said and lifted my chin, forcing me to look at him. "I love you, Soph."

Later that day he dropped me at Blockbuster to pick up some movies. I headed straight for the new releases. It was a lazy Sunday, and I drifted along the aisle, looking at the covers and admiring my ring every time it caught the light. I went to grab a DVD and simultaneously someone else's hand went for the same one.

"Sorry," I said, turning to the person next to me.

"Sorry," she said at exactly the same time. "Hi, Sophie."

"Oh, hi."

Mia and me, face to face after all this time of not talking. It defined awkward.

"What are you doing?" I blundered, even though it was obvious.

"Getting a movie." She nodded her head toward the cover in my hand. "I've seen that."

"Any good?"

She screwed up her nose. "Remember that hideous film we saw on holiday last year?"

"Yeah," I said, "the kung fu one." It was on a trip down south with my parents, one of those holidays where it seemed like all we did was swim and eat and laugh. We'd gone to this film night in an old church and seen the worst Chinese action movie ever made. The whole way through, Mia did a voice-over like a kung fu expert, making me and the only other two people there laugh hysterically for the whole ninety minutes.

"That's right," she said, smiling. "It's not as good as that."

I laughed and stuck it back on the shelf. "Think I'll give it a pass."

And then the awkwardness descended rapidly. The familiarity of her was like an electric jolt, nostalgia and regret all swirled up together. There was so much to say, but instead I couldn't meet her eye again.

"Well," she said, holding out the DVD we'd both reached for, "do you want this one then?"

"No, you have it. I'll get something else."

"Okay." She moved her weight from one foot to the other. "Okay then."

"Okay then," I repeated.

"See you," she said and moved to the counter.

"Bye." I turned away and blinked back the tears.

mia

I lived in Boredomland. Every other weekend I watched Jordie go off to Dad's. Dad wanted me to come too, but I couldn't. I heard Mom warn him on the phone to give me some space, that I'd broken up with my boyfriend and needed to be left alone. She did the same, spending hours with Damon at his house on the weekend. I truly was alone.

I'd walk from room to room overwhelmed with bleakness. I wanted to scream and break things. Rip my hair out or smash my reflection in the mirror. Some days I didn't get out of bed. I'd lie there thinking about how I deserved everything I got. How I should just die. Every day I hated myself more. I'd had it all, and I'd thrown it all away. Now I had nothing and no one.

Seeing Sophie at Blockbuster–her happiness and familiarity–made everything worse. I hated myself for wasting our friendship. It used to be Soph and me, renting movies and having fun together, but now that had all changed and it was all my fault.

I knew I'd never have another friend like Sophie. I needed some type of human contact, even if it was only cyber. I went into a couple of chat rooms. I saw a forum on drug use and typed in "ecstasy."

I skipped over the heavy stories—the side effects and long-term damage—and read the happy stuff. Reading those stories was like turning on a light. I wasn't alone. There were other people just like me who'd found themselves through drugs. I wasn't abnormal. I wasn't the only person in the world feeling this way. There were lots of people out there just like me.

It hit me hard. It was a wonderful experience. The stories I read took me right back into the beauty of it all— the peace, love, and unity. Why had I stopped? I'd always had it under control. It wasn't like I'd been using every day. Or couldn't stop if I wanted to. I shook my head in disbelief. I'd fallen for all the hype and scare tactics. I couldn't believe what an idiot I'd been. Tower had died because he was a hard-core doper. He was reckless, an extreme case. He didn't know what was in half the stuff he took and he'd take anything he could get his hands on. The more thought I gave it, the clearer it became. Lewis was right. Nothing he or Roger or I could have done would have helped Tower.

I wasn't like Tower. I didn't mix drugs, apart from the occasional line of coke. And a bit of weed, to bring myself down. And weed isn't a chemical anyway–it grows naturally. My Es always came from a reliable source and I'd never had a bad experience. For the first time in weeks I smiled. Why was I sitting here depressed when I could be having fun?

He picked up the phone on the second ring.

"Hi there."

"It's Mia." I was a bit nervous. "What's going on?"

"Not a lot." He sounded lethargic. "Got a few friends around, chilling out."

"Oh," I paused. I wasn't sure how to ask–I'd never had to before.

"Wanna come over?" he asked before I could speak.

"Yeah," I said gratefully.

"I'll pick you up in fifteen."

I brushed my hair and looked at myself in the mirror. It's okay, I told my reflection, you know you can stop whenever you want. You've been three weeks without it. I heard him pull up in the driveway, grabbed my purse and cell, and ran outside.

I slid into the front seat. The car stank of cigarette smoke and was littered with fast food containers.

We headed down the street, his arm draped over the back of my seat. I looked at him out of the corner of my eye. He was kind of attractive in an unshaven sort of way.

My foot tapped against the floor. Phoning Glenn had seemed like a good idea, but now I wasn't so sure. "How's everyone doing?" I said suddenly, to break the silence.

"Yeah, okay." He lit a cigarette and hung his arm out the window. "Bit of a shock, Tower dying like that. But you know, you get that." He shrugged his shoulders. "He always used to say, 'Live fast, die young.'"

"Yeah, but I don't think he really meant it."

"You didn't know Tower like we did." Glenn flicked ash out the window. We sat without speaking for a minute.

I had to say something. "About Sophie," I began, but he cut me off by swerving off the road into a parking lot. He turned the ignition off and grabbed my hand.

"Look at me, Mia," he ordered.

Suddenly I was terrified. Alone, in a car with this guy I barely knew. Maybe even a rapist. What the hell was I thinking? I swallowed hard and looked at him. He squeezed my hand tightly.

"I have never, ever forced myself on anyone in my life." As he spoke a bit of spit flew off his lip and hit my cheek. I was too scared to pull my hand away and wipe it off. "You know I like Sophie. She's fun and easygoing. But she has to take responsibility. What she did was her choice." His dark eyes bored into me. I couldn't look away.

"We went back to my place and we got it on. I swear to God, Mia, she wasn't raped or set up. There was no gang bang. She chose to do everything she did. And I guess now she wants to blame someone."

I believed him. I knew Soph, and she did do crazy stuff if she'd had too much to drink. Later she always blamed it on being out of it, not responsible. She'd be the same on drugs. This was the Thomas Westcroft episode all over again. She was just making excuses.

"Yeah," I said finally.

He nodded and turned on the ignition. I hesitated for one second. Part of me said, Don't do it.

"Got any Es?"

"Got any cash?" Glenn asked as we headed down the street again.

"Nah." I opened my purse. "But I've got my ATM card."

sophie

Dom knew something was wrong when he picked me up outside Blockbuster.

"What's up?" he asked, reversing out of the lot.

I couldn't speak and tried to stop the tears sliding down my cheeks.

"Hey." He pulled off the road. "Where's the happy girl I left fifteen minutes ago?"

"I saw Mia," I said and burst into tears.

He held my hand as I cried. I told him everything—absolutely everything. And it was weird, but the truth—about Thomas Westcroft and feeling like I had this stupid reputation to keep up—flowed from me freely. He didn't say much, but he didn't need to. He put his arm around me as I cried and blurted out what I'd done over the last couple of years. "And why would you even want to be with me now?" I said, wiping my nose, sure I looked horrible. But he just smiled again and squeezed me tighter.

"Sophie, we all make mistakes," he said. "I just like being with you. It'll all be okay."

But later, when we sat watching the movie, I couldn't stop thinking about Mia. She was the sister I'd never had. What had she done that was so wrong? Dom was right; we all make mistakes. I had to come clean. It was time to be honest with her too.

Tomorrow was my birthday; I was turning sixteen. Mom and Dad were taking me out for dinner, my brothers were coming, and of course Dom would be there. It was going to be a special night. But it would only be perfect if I could make up with Mia and have her there too.

mia

Glenn stopped at an ATM and I withdrew two hundred bucks, a chunk of my savings. I gave him the money. Es cost forty bucks each, so I figured I'd just bought myself five.

We parked outside a large block of old apartments and I followed Glenn up cracked concrete steps to his place. The living room was small and stuffy and dark. Through an archway I saw the tiny kitchen, every counter loaded with dirty dishes and empty wrappers and cartons. There was the smell of greasy bacon fat mixed with weed and stale cigarettes in the air. Through another doorway I saw a bedroom, with crumpled and balled-up clothes on the floor.

Glenn had left his friends to get me, and they were still there when we got back, sitting on a torn couch with their feet resting on a battered wooden chest among half-empty beer bottles and overflowing ashtrays. One of them looked up at me, but no one said anything. Loud music thumped out of huge speakers. There were lava lamps circulating gigantic blobs of viscous pink liquid up and down inside their watery centers, and party lights, tiny flashing blue-and-silver bulbs that winked and blinked.

Glenn disappeared into his bedroom and I stood awkward and uncomfortable, pretending to be interested in the flashing lights. To my relief he came back soon, carrying a plastic bag with five pills in it. He gave me two pills, took two himself, and put the other one in his pocket. I was surprised, but didn't say anything. I figured what goes around comes around; I'd had plenty of freebies before. No big deal.

Twenty minutes later I felt the E taking effect. It was a familiar, welcome feeling, and I embraced it. Instantly I became confident and started talking to Glenn. The other guys eventually left, but Glenn and I were too deep in conversation to pay them any attention. We talked about Lewis and Tower and then he told me about his feelings for me.

"You know, Mia, the first time I laid eyes on you I thought you were beautiful."

I laughed. "I bet you say that to all the girls."

"Nah, it's true. You're a special person."

Our eyes locked and I couldn't break away. We sat for an eternity staring into each other's eyes. And the most amazing thing happened. His face began to morph and change into different people. Not people I knew, but strangers, hundreds of strangers. In his irises, I watched the core of humanity swirl by. I saw the history of the world: past, present, and future. We were all a part of each other's existence. I belonged to a universal consciousness.

"It's amazing," he said finally.

I nodded my head, awed by the special thing we'd just shared, then I lost myself in the happiness of being back where I belonged.

I stayed the night at Glenn's. It was awesome to feel the touch of someone else again, and he dropped me home at six, before Mom got in.

sophie

I called Mia's cell, but it went to voice mail. What I wanted to say couldn't be left as a recording or a text, so I waited to see her at school the next morning.

It was difficult to sleep that night, imagining the conversation we might have. And when I awoke it was with an awareness that something important was going to happen. I felt slightly nervous, but happy too at the idea of turning everything around.

I waited outside her homeroom, but she didn't come. I waited until the first bell sounded and the hallways were deserted before I sprinted to my own class.

At lunch I went to our bench. She was a small crouched figure sitting in the hallway, doodling in the notebook on her lap.

"Hi," I said, nervous that she might tell me to piss off

or something. She looked up slowly. She looked tired and kind of sad.

"Hi," she said flatly.

The conversation I'd rehearsed all night was already unraveling. I hadn't expected this. The day before she'd seemed wistful, nostalgic even.

"Whatchya doing?" I didn't want to give up immediately. I'd done enough of that.

"Nothing," she said, looking at me blankly. It was like all the life had drained out of her. What on earth could've happened between last night and now?

"Have you forgotten what today is?" I asked.

She squinted and assessed me before flicking her eyes away. "Happy birthday, Soph."

It was so wrong, but I couldn't give up. "I miss you, Mia." She wasn't looking at me, she was just staring vacantly at the drawings in her notebook. "I hate the way things are." She wouldn't look up. "And I owe you an apology."

"Yeah?" Finally she looked at me.

"I blamed you for everything going wrong, but it was my fault too. I lied to you and I'm so sorry." I didn't want to cry, but she was making this so hard. Why wouldn't she give me some response? Something, anything, would be better than this silence. "I lied about so many things, right from the beginning of last year. I've never done it with anyone. Ever. I made that up, everything. I don't know why." Tears streamed down my cheeks. I wanted to hug her and feel some warmth. "I'm so sorry."

"Is that it?" She shrugged. "So what?"

"Yeah, no, I ..." I was stunned by her response. I don't know what the hell I'd been expecting, but it definitely wasn't this. I thought she'd jump at the chance to make up and be friends again. I thought she'd care that I was sorry. I was wrong. "Yeah, well, I just thought I'd tell you that. And say hi. So, hi and, well, see you then."

"See ya," she said, head down, continuing to draw.

And I didn't have to look at the picture to know that it was some drug icon. It was so obvious what had happened.

mia

I was dreading my report. My big drop in marks would be glaringly obvious, and then there'd be tons of explaining to do. But it was just impossible to concentrate. My brain wouldn't focus for any length of time, no matter how hard I tried. I couldn't even keep my attention on TV. I'd have to get up and walk around. At school I'd sit listening to my iPod, to the music that took me back to the weekends. Music was the only thing I could focus on. I wanted to write it all down in a diary, but I was terrified of Mom finding it and reading it. I wouldn't put it past her to go through my things, which was why I was so careful about hiding stuff, like my Es, weed, and contraceptive pills.

It was getting to be a real pain with Mom, and Jordie too. I couldn't relate to them on any level. We didn't connect. Each day brought me closer to the weekend, where I belonged. Not that I did Es every night of the weekend, I couldn't afford to. But knowing I'd be back in that zone made the week bearable.

Most of the time Mom and I would pass each other in the kitchen. I'd leave the fridge door open and she'd kick it shut. I'd go straight to my room after dinner. I was starting to feel paranoid around her. I didn't like the way she watched me, like she was on the verge of saying something.

I was sitting at the kitchen table drinking juice when I heard her footsteps. I jumped up quickly to leave the room, but she leaned in the doorway, looking at me. Glenn had been around a few times to pick me up and she didn't like him. That much was obvious.

"Tell me, what happened between you and Lewis?" she finally asked.

"It just ended," I said, irritated. I didn't want to discuss my life. She still had no idea about Tower.

"He seemed like such a nice boy."

I felt like laughing. She was so shallow, judging Glenn by his appearance, his crappy car, his lack of a job, but he wasn't so different from Lewis. In fact, really he was more honest because he didn't hide behind some bullshit image.

"Glenn seems"–she paused–"a little old for you."

"He's only nineteen."

"But you're not sixteen yet," she said tersely.

I sighed heavily. Why did she always have to go on at me? "Four weeks, Mom. In four weeks I will be and then I'll be able to leave here if I want," I threatened. I hated the way she tried to control me.

"Mia, what's got into you?" Her tone had changed. The anger had gone and she sounded sad.

"You," I shouted. "Now I know why Dad left. You were always trying to tell him what to do too." I got up and pushed past her. I didn't want to see her face; I knew she'd be crying. But why wouldn't she leave me alone? I didn't question her about where she went and what she did.

After that, every morning she would corner and interrogate me. I didn't know why she was showing this sudden interest in my life, but I didn't like it. Too late, Mom, I wanted to scream at her.

A couple of days later it was, "I haven't seen Sophie for a long time."

"Yeah." My best defense, I found, was to give monosyllabic replies.

"Did you two have a fight?"

"Mmm." I pretended to read a magazine.

"But you've been best friends forever." She pulled out a

chair and sat down. She was starting to really get to me. Back off, Mom.

"People change," I snapped. "You should know that."

"Mia, is everything all right?" she asked suddenly.

"Yep," I said. My brain was racing. She was making me nervous. Had she found something?

"You haven't seemed happy lately." She reached across and touched my hand.

I almost snorted. I'd never been so happy in my entire life. Well, not here in this house, with the interrogator, but when I was at Glenn's I was truly happy.

"I'm fine, Mom. Look, I've got to go. I'll be late for school."

I got up to leave. She was watching me so intently I felt kind of freaked out.

"You know I love you," she said.

It sounded so bizarre and unnatural that I hid my face and almost ran out of the room.

I'd told myself I wouldn't touch pills on weeknights. It was hard enough to get up for school as it was. But a weird thing was happening. I was getting more and more depressed. Mom's new interest was making me paranoid and jittery, and even when I was rolling I couldn't shake those negative feelings. It worried me. I felt like I was losing the inner peace that ecstasy gave me.

After Mom's declaration of love I didn't want to go home. I was sure she was onto something. I didn't know what, but I could feel a deep and meaningful conversation coming on and I wanted to avoid it.

So I went to Glenn's after school. It was the same scene as usual, a couple of other people sitting around, chilling out. I guess I was pretty naive, but it had taken me a while to figure out that Glenn was a dealer. All the "friends" that dropped by were either scoring from Glenn or dealing to him. The lighting was always dim, the party lights flashing, and the music loud. Anything was available at Glenn's: GHB, LSD, ice, and heroin—gear I found scary. I had a handle on Es and coke—weed didn't even count—but I didn't want to progress any further.

Even though Glenn was my boyfriend now, nothing was free. He'd give me the occasional one, but most of the time I bought my own stuff. He had to pay his supplier too. My savings were nearly gone, and that worried me. When the money ran out, what would I do?

So this was my frame of mind when I decided not to go home from school. Glenn was happy to see me, which wasn't always the case when I showed up unannounced. He was in a generous mood, and when he offered me a freebie, even though it was a Wednesday night, I didn't hesitate. I wanted something to lift my blackness.

I was chilling out when Mom called my cell at about six, sounding totally frantic. "Where are you?" she demanded.

"At Glenn's," I said simply.

"It's a school night, Mia." She was completely pissed off. But the E had kicked in and I was feeling mellow, so I tried to reason with her.

"I'll be home by ten," I said, knowing it was untrue.

"I'm coming to get you," she said angrily. "What's the address?"

The idea of her knowing where he lived frightened me. "If you come here," I threatened, "I'll run away and you won't ever see me again."

She was waiting for me in the kitchen when I got home early on Thursday morning. "We need to talk," she said firmly. So much for avoiding things. "You're out of control, Mia."

I shrugged.

"You're fifteen," she said sadly, "too young to stay out at night and do whatever you want to do."

I crossed my arms watching her. She was such a small person, scurrying around wiping countertops. Her whole object in life was to tell me what to do—when it suited her. And when she wanted to be free of me, I was old enough to stay home alone. I despised her with a passion. Her mouth kept moving, blah, blah, blah. I wished she'd shut up, but she went on, her hands waving, her eyes filled with tears, and it was suddenly amusing. She was this funny, insular little creature, with lots to say about nothing.

"I don't even like this boy Glenn. He's too old for you. Why can't he get a girl his own age? What he's doing is illegal, and I could have him arrested."

Those words jolted me. What did she know about Glenn? Who'd told her? She was quiet, waiting for a response, sensing that her words had struck home. But then I realized she wasn't talking about drugs—she was talking about sex. Her despicable little threat was about reporting him for having sex with a minor. Hatred for her engulfed me, this boring little woman with her narrow, shallow ideas.

"You hypocrite," I spat venomously. She'd been fifteen when she started having sex. She told me so herself, back in the days when we had those mother-daughter talks where she was preparing me for the future. "If you ever do anything like that I'll never speak to you again," I warned. "Ever."

I turned and walked out of the room. Inwardly I was shaking, surprised by the things I'd felt and said. We were heading into dangerous territory. Something was about to give.

She followed me to my room, like a dog with a bone.

"You're not going out this weekend," she said, standing in my doorway, hands on her hips. "You're grounded."

She was so pathetic. She nearly made me laugh.

"Yeah, right, just try it."

"I mean it, Mia." The strain of trying not to shout made her visibly vibrate. "You're not going anywhere this weekend, or the next."

"You can't stop me." Who did she think she was? Interfering control freak. "Stop trying to ruin my life."

"I'm your mother, whether you like it or not." She was shouting now, completely losing it. And then she held her hand up to stop me walking through the door. "I can stop you–I have the law on my side."

She was a bully and a coward. I hated her!

"Get out of my way." I knocked her arm away. I'm taller than she is, and stronger.

"Mia, don't." She grabbed at me.

"Let go of me," I snarled at her. "I hate you. Let go of me." I shrugged out of her grip and then shoved her hard into the doorframe.

She slapped me. The sound of it resonated like an echo. My cheek stung. I was shocked. In all my life my mother had never hit me.

"Fuck off," I spat at her. She looked horrified and was crying too. "You can't make me stay." I pushed past her, grabbed my bag, and ran out the door.

At Glenn's I had to drop a pill to calm down. I needed to zone out. Chill. Later, I tried to explain to him what happened.

"Fuck, Mia. She'll come here," he said, looking around.

"No, she won't. She doesn't know where you live."

"Are you going back?"

"No way." I knew I couldn't stay at Glenn's. She'd have him charged for sex with a minor if I moved in. That was the sort of vindictive thing she'd do to get back at me. "I'm going to call my dad."

sophie

After that I washed my hands of her. Everything that Mia had once been, all those things about her I'd admired and loved, were being eroded by drugs. There was nothing whatever that I could do to change or even stop what was happening. Worst of all was hearing through the school grapevine that she was with Glenn. No matter what she thought of me, you'd think she would have heeded something, one tiny thing of what I'd said. The idea of her having sex with him in that disgusting, filthy flat made me want to throw up.

But Dominic was worried about her and wanted me to try to get through to her.

"You don't get it, Dom. She won't talk to me. She doesn't want help. You can't help those who won't help themselves," I said. There is only so much a person can do. If she wanted to ruin her life, that was her choice.

mia

Dad seemed relieved to hear from me. I figured Mom had already called him and probably blamed him for the way I was behaving. I think he was pleased to be put in the position of rescuer. He said I could move in with him and Kylie. It seemed like my best option.

When I got home Damon's car was in the driveway. He and Mom were in the kitchen sharing a bottle of wine. They both looked pained when I walked in.

"Mia, I'm so sorry," Mom said, jumping up and approaching me.

I put my hand up to stop her. "Don't," I warned. "I've had enough."

"I shouldn't have hit you." Mom was trying not to cry, but it didn't interest me. Her emotional blackmail wouldn't work on me anymore.

"I'm going," I said, and the tears started to roll down her face.

"Please, don't do this."

"Why, Mom? It's better for all of us. I'm always in the way anyhow. Reminding you of the big mistake you made." She flinched like I'd hit her. It made me almost smile. Then I delivered my final blow. "I'm going to live with Dad." I slammed the door behind me, but I could still hear her crying.

I was going through my wardrobe, packing clothes into a suitcase. I didn't have a lot to wear. I suddenly realized how much weight I'd lost—nearly all my clothes were way too big for me. I picked out the smallest things I had. Barely half a suitcase.

"Mia?" It was Jordie. He was standing in my doorway, head down and crying.

"Hey, Jord, what's wrong?" I sat on the edge of the bed and held my hand out to him. I didn't like to see him cry. It reminded me of bad times.

"Why are you going away?" he asked, sniffing loudly.

"I can't stay here anymore," I said, holding his hand. "It'll be okay, Jord."

"But I don't want you to go. You promised me."

I had promised him. When Dad walked out and Jordie

cried and cried about how Dad didn't love us anymore, I promised, no matter what, that he and I would stay together.

"I'm only going to Dad's," I said brightly. "We'll be together on the weekends you come. Please don't cry."

"But you're never around. I never see you anymore."

"Things'll be different at Dad's. I promise."

Dad and Kylie live in a street of new townhouses interspersed with perfectly clipped hedges and jacarandas. It was part of Dad's change of life. When he left Mom he got rid of his old self for a new one. He traded his four-door sedan for a two-door sports car, and the wife and kids for a slightly younger, childless woman.

Kylie was putting on a good face. I doubted she wanted me there, but she'd do anything for Dad. Be nice to the kids and he won't leave. Because if he could walk out on his own flesh and blood, what real hold did she have over him?

She gave me the downstairs bedroom with its bland carpet and cream walls. It was completely different from my room at home. Mom had let me do whatever I liked there, so I painted it orange and pink, and Mom bought me sheets and a duvet cover in the same colors, shot through with gold. I had cushions scattered everywhere, and scented candles. I used to love my room. But this one suited me fine. I didn't care what it looked like. At least when I came home late I wouldn't have to walk up the stairs and past their bedroom. Jordie would keep the room we'd shared on the top floor, so I had my privacy. Sweet.

"I thought maybe tonight we could all go out to dinner," Kylie suggested, watching me put my things away.

"I've got plans," I said. Which was not true, but I hoped Glenn would be happy to see me anyway.

She was quiet, not knowing what to say. Trying to be the interested quasi-stepmother, which, thanks very much, I didn't need. I already had one mother too many.

"Maybe another night," I offered, wanting her to go away.

Later, as I was getting ready to go out, I heard her and Dad talking.

"Don't push her, Kylie," he warned. "She's not going to be your friend straightaway. Give her some time."

I looked at myself in the mirror. Good, I thought, Dad'll help keep her off my back.

sophie

Mia dropped off the radar. In the weeks that followed she took days off school at a time. When she did turn up it was like she was vanishing. She was thinner than I'd ever seen and her skin looked awful.

It drove me mental that I still kept thinking about her, wondering where she was, if she was safe, how much she was using. It scared me to think about what she might be taking now. Sometimes I thought about calling her mom and telling her everything I knew, but then I'd be betraying her, and for what? I didn't know what to do.

In every other respect life was great. I'd spend most of my time with Dom. And it was strange how now the pressure was off me I was so more relaxed in doing the things we did. He was happy to go as far as I wanted and never made me feel like a tease if I stopped. And even though he had exams coming up, I still saw him. I spent heaps of time at his house. And my mom didn't even mind. Dom's dad taught me chess, and told me stories about his travels that made me want to do something real. Maybe work in a Third World country myself. I wanted to help people. If the irony of this escapes you, don't worry, I didn't see it either until it was almost too late.

mia

Kylie did as she was told and left me alone. I went to Glenn's every night and most times didn't bother going back to Dad's. I was skipping school a lot, and I knew it wouldn't be long before they started phoning, but Dad wasn't on my case. It wasn't hard to convince him that I was at school, or at Sophie's, and that all the drama was in Mom's head. He'd make comments about me being skinny and needing to eat more, but he never went any further than that. Finally, I had some space.

My birthday was coming up and Dad wanted to organize something. He told me I could invite my friends over, but when I looked at the white sofas and glass-top coffee tables and pictured Glenn and his dirty feet, I couldn't see it working.

"What about we just do something with the four of us," I suggested. Dad looked pretty pleased that I'd included Kylie.

"Okay," he said, pulling out his wallet, "you go and organize a cake."

Typical Dad. His idea of doing something for my birthday was to supply the money. But then he handed me his ATM card. As I took it from him, my heart was racing with relief and anxiety.

"The PIN is 9486," he said. "Use the savings account."

The thin card felt as heavy as a revolver in my hand.

"Oh, and Mia," he said as he walked out of the room, "buy yourself something for your birthday. Maybe some clothes?"

I couldn't look at him. All I felt was the piece of plastic in my hand.

One day during the first week at Dad's I'd come back from Glenn's to find both Dad and Kylie out. I walked through the house looking at their things. Really looking. Everything in the house was Kylie—oriental pots and weird abstract art—and I couldn't see my dad in any of it. The stuff was a world away from the dad I used to live with. He was a huge Formula One fan and he had signed photographs of Grand Prix drivers crossing the finish line. He had piles of books too, on deep-sea fishing and California flora.

My dad loved gardening. At the end of the day he'd walk around outside, a beer in his hand, watching his plants grow. Here, they had a tiny paved courtyard with cacti growing in pots. He didn't have a study; a flat screen computer sat in an alcove with coffee table books on French houses and European interiors.

Dad used to drink beer, but now he drinks dry martinis, the same as Kylie. They go to cafés and the theater. I was interested in my dad's reinvention, even though it hurt. I walked around picking up photos of them on a skiing holiday together, a holiday Jordie and I hadn't been invited to. I opened drawers and looked inside highly polished, deep blue pots.

Snooping around through their stuff, I found loads of loose change. Every pot or drawer had money in it, and I even found a fifty dollar bill at the back of a drawer full of receipts and stuff. I held it in my hand and knew I couldn't not take it. It was as simple as that. My account was dry, my stash was gone—and here was some money. Glenn was pretty stingy. If I didn't have the cash, I didn't get a pill. I was taking less of them than ever before and finding it more and more difficult to reach nirvana. So I pocketed the fifty. They probably didn't even know it was there. I didn't feel particularly guilty—they have plenty of money.

But fifty bucks doesn't go far, not when a pill costs forty–

well, twenty for me. Over the next three weeks I pretty much raided all the pots and drawers of their coins. Not completely though. I'd leave a few coins around so the drawers didn't look too empty. And I'd sold a few things–to Glenn and some of his dealer friends, mostly the gifts that Lewis had given me when he was trying to impress me with his wealth. But things of value were difficult to come by.

And then Dad handed me his card and PIN.

I went to the bakery and ordered a cake. I used the card and asked the girl for extra cash. She didn't even look at the name on it, just gave me the fifty bucks. It was too easy. Dad would happily believe the cake was eighty dollars.

Then I went to Jean Machine and bought a couple of pairs of jeans. Size eight was way too big now and I fit into a four. When I looked at myself in the mirror I felt pretty pleased with my appearance. I bought a couple of tops too, and got a cash advance of a hundred. By the end of the day I had a cake on order, new gear to wear, and a hundred and fifty bucks in my pocket.

I knew I needed to be careful with the money. I bought a stash from Glenn that I hid in my bedroom, but I was already worrying about what I'd do once that ran out.

sophie

When things first started going missing no one gave it a lot of thought. It happens. People lose stuff, or if they're careless and leave it lying around someone will take it. It was a couple of iPods to start with, then some cell phones, and later some purses. It soon became obvious there was a major thief among us.

Staff started watching students closely and the thefts eased up, but only for a week or so. The school was plastered with posters telling everyone to Keep Valuables Safe and Report Suspicious People to Admin. It was kind of like a terrorist alert. Everyone was suspicious of anyone behaving strangely.

Mia seemed to escape scrutiny, maybe because she was hardly ever at school, but I know now that if we'd cross-referenced her days at school with the days when there were thefts, there would've been a perfect match.

I know this because Mia was the thief. She took my purse and accessed my cash card. So what idiot tells someone their PIN? But in the old days I told Mia everything, and even when we weren't friends anymore it never occurred to me in a million years that she would steal from me.

The cops found my purse in a dumpster near the mall. She took out five hundred bucks, though she could have taken more. My balance at the time was over five thousand, money I'd inherited from my grandmother. She could've taken up to a grand there and then, but she didn't. The cops asked me to look at the security video and I watched the way she hid her face from the camera. It was a blurred and grainy image, but I had no doubt it was Mia. Her fingers hit the buttons quickly and her head darted around several times. But she never looked at the camera—it was like someone had told her where the camera was—and she pocketed the cash quickly. It filled me with revulsion to see what she'd become. A thief. Stealing from me.

"No," I told the cops, "I don't know who it is."

"But this person knows your number." The cop looked at me skeptically. "Who've you told?"

I looked him in the eye. "No one. I had it written

down in my purse. I know it was dumb, but it could have been worse, it could have been thousands." I shrugged as if relieved. The cop looked at me like I was the stupidest person he'd ever met.

mia

The day before my birthday I came home to find Kylie in my room. She hadn't heard me come in because she was too busy looking through my drawers. All my books were on the floor. She'd obviously flicked through the pages searching for something. It takes a cunning bitch to think like that. I leaned against the doorway watching her. I darted a quick look at the photo of me and Dad and Jordie—its heavy Indonesian box frame has plenty of room at the back to hide a stash—but she hadn't touched it. So I was pretty relaxed as I watched her go through my things, thinking how much I'd like to punch her in the face.

Eventually she looked up and saw me. Her eyes nearly popped out of her head and she went bright red.

"So," I said, calmly, "did you find it?"

She got up from the floor and wiped her hands nervously down her white pants. I hate white pants.

"What?" she said, nervously.

223

"Whatever it is you're looking for." I felt the anger bubbling up in me, from way down deep in the pit of my stomach.

"Ah, Mia …" She shook her head, finding it difficult to speak.

"Get out of my room!" I screamed at her. The rage surged up with such ferocity it took me by surprise. She was backed against the wall and couldn't get out because I was blocking the way.

"You stupid, nosy slut," I screamed even louder. "How dare you? You think it's okay to ruin a family. To steal a father from his children. What right do you have, Kylie? What fucking right?"

I think she was frightened I was going to hit her. And maybe I was. I'd never felt such rage before. She was crying.

"I thought –" she began.

"Get out of my room, you stupid bitch." I didn't want to hear anything she had to say. I took a step toward her. "Get out!" I screamed as her white ass disappeared down the hallway.

I locked the door. I knew Dad wasn't going to let me get away with that, so I prepared myself. I didn't want to have a fight with him. I unscrewed the back of the frame and took out my stash. I had one pill left, which I was saving for my birthday. I took it and waited. I was glad I'd finally told Kylie exactly what I thought of her. She knew, when she went into business with Dad, that he was married, that he had two kids, and she still set out to get him. Seduced him through e-mails and text messages, by wearing short skirts and flaunting her body at him. What chance did Mom have? And I hated what she'd turned my dad into—some pompous try-hard who thought he was young and trendy. I was glad I'd taken her money, and her jewelry. She had no morals. She stole husbands, and that was far worse than anything I'd done.

I listened to his car pull up, heard the garage door open. A slam, footsteps, and then the low murmur of voices. I heard her wail, "Matthew …" She doesn't call him Matt, like everyone else. And then more soft voices and crying. Cry a river of tears, you bitch, I thought, like me, Jordie, and Mom did when Dad walked out.

I was waiting for Dad. I'd started something and I wanted to finish it. The E was my truth serum. Bring it on, Dad.

"Mia?" His knock on the door was gentle but his voice was stern.

"What?" I asked pleasantly.

"I want to talk to you." He rattled the doorknob. "Unlock this door."

"What, Dad?" I asked innocently as I opened the door.

"You know." He looked angry. Now this was interesting, watching Dad deal with someone's hurt feelings. "You've really upset Kylie."

"I know." I sat on the bed and he sat next to me. "But she was in here, snooping through my stuff."

"She's worried about you –"

"Give me a break." How dare he take her side? "I don't want to hear any of that crap. She's a devious, manipulative bitch."

"Stop it," he warned, really angry. "She agreed to you coming here. She was more than happy to have you live here."

I sat there with my mouth open, staring at Dad like he had just told me he was a cross-dresser. What was he saying?

"Right," I muttered, "I should feel grateful that the slut who stole my father allows me to live in his house with him? Go figure, Dad." I got up off the bed. I didn't want to talk to him anymore. I wanted to get out of there.

"She thinks you might be using drugs," Dad said after a moment.

I glared at him like I couldn't believe what he was saying. "And you'd believe her, wouldn't you? You'd believe her over your own daughter?" I was hysterical. It was a waste of an E. I'd totally come down. He'd spoiled that for me too.

"She thinks you've taken money and jewelry. And accessed our bank account," he said quite gently. I couldn't even speak. Tears were filling my eyes and nose.

"I can't believe you." I wiped at my face. "I'm not staying here."

"No," he said. "If this is going to work you've got to live by some rules."

"And what rules are those, Dad?" I shouted at him. "The ones you make up as you go along? If you don't like the deal, just leave. Isn't that what you did?"

"Mia," he said, grabbing my arm.

"Don't," I snapped at him. "It's a bit late to start being the concerned father."

By the time I got to Glenn's I felt like everything was unraveling. I didn't belong anywhere. No one wanted me. No one loved me. What had happened to me?

"Hey, calm down," he said, taking me into the bedroom and out of sight of the guys in the living room. "What's happening?"

I told him about Kylie going through my stuff, and the fight with Dad, but he wasn't interested. He kept looking at the door like he'd rather be out there.

"Here," he said, pulling out a couple of pills, "you need to forget it, babe, and chill out."

In a little while I was able to view the situation more rationally. I lay next to Glenn on the bed and now he listened to me. He completely empathized when I explained to him what my parents had been doing.

"They don't understand you, Mia," he said. "They're trying to get you to fit into their lives without allowing you to be yourself."

He was right. That's exactly what they'd been doing to me. Pushing and pulling, using me to wage war against each other, not caring about my feelings in the slightest. I felt all the sadness pouring out of me. I cried until I was empty. I never wanted to leave.

Mom and Dad both texted me that night, but I deleted their messages. And then Mom kept calling. Finally I decided to answer, just to tell her to back off.

"What do you want?"

"What's happening?" she cried. "Please tell me."

"I can't talk to you," I said.

"Please come home. Please, Mia."

"No," I said. "I don't have a home. Not with you and not with him."

"Are you doing drugs?" she finally asked.

Dad had been whispering in her ear too.

"No," I shouted into my cell. "That's so typical, Mom. You can't handle the fact I've left because of the way you treat me, so it has to be something else, doesn't it? And Dad didn't leave you because Kylie enticed him away. He left because you're a control freak."

I switched my phone off. For a moment I wondered if she'd try to find me, but she didn't know the address, and anyway, she's not really the type. She loathes confrontation. I was surprised she'd even called.

sophie

I finally did it. After my interview with the police I went to Mia's house and told her mom everything. Dom came with me. Things had spiraled out of control, but I had a weird feeling too that somewhere deep inside, a bit of the old Mia remained. She could've cleaned out my entire account. A true desperado druggie with no regard for anyone else would have. But she didn't. I was sure it was a cry for help.

In front of my eyes her mother disintegrated.

"Sophie, Sophie …" She grabbed my hand tightly. "Why didn't you tell me before?"

I shook my head, ashamed.

Dom squeezed my knee under the table. "This isn't Sophie's fault, Mrs. Larson. She tried to help."

I smiled at Dom through my tears. "I'm really sorry,

Rae. I didn't know what to do. But things are getting pretty bad. I think she could be in real danger."

All this time, Mia had been out there on her own, barreling towards self-destruction while everyone stood around and passively watched. Now we were all trying to find her, but it wasn't easy. Presumably she was at Glenn's. A familiar feeling of horror crawled up my body as I recalled his flat.

After several texts and phone calls Mia finally picked up. Dom and I sat listening to Rae's end of the conversation. It sounded like Mia was mad as hell. I heard her voice, hard and irate through the speakerphone. Rae tried to calm her, but then she blew it. As soon as I heard her ask the question I knew what would happen. Mia flew into a rage and denied it all. Denial. Denial. From the phone's speaker I heard the raging fury and then the hang-up.

"Where?" her mom asked me, her eyes bright shiny discs in a white face. "Where does he live?"

I shook my head. I knew the bus stop, but I wasn't sure exactly where we went from there.

Then I remembered. "Lewis Scott. He'll know."

Dom got hold of a number for Lewis and rang him, but Lewis said he had no idea where Glenn lived. He'd never been to his place.

"Dom, have you got any idea at all?" I said desperately. "You picked me up."

"I know where I picked you up from, Soph, but it was in the middle of a shopping district."

We drove out with Rae and Damon. Dom pulled into the parking lot of a fast food outlet and we all got out. He pointed to a lamppost.

"There's where you were," he said. "Do you know which direction you came from?"

I held Dom's hand. The area's seediness and desperation creeped me out. "No, but we weren't far from the river. It stank. But …" I looked around. None of it was familiar at all. "I'm so sorry," I said to Rae, "I've got no idea."

"It's okay," she said, hugging me tightly. "It's okay."

Dom drove around a bit, but no landmarks were familiar, and we eventually went back to Rae's house, then sat and waited for the phone to ring. We sent Mia messages, but she never responded. She wouldn't call. I knew she would've turned her phone off. What were we waiting for? At eleven Dom took me home.

"I'll call you if I hear anything," Rae said as we left.

"It's her birthday tomorrow," I said stupidly.

"I know," her mom said. "I think I'll have to call the police then."

mia

My birthday. Sweet sixteen.

I was completely down and struggling to get happy, even on the two Es I'd taken. Nothing worked. I walked around the flat, chugging one glass of rum and Coke after another. I wasn't even slightly drunk. In fact, the Es and alcohol seemed to make my mood worse. The black hole was getting deeper. I felt sadder and sadder until I couldn't stand it anymore.

"What's wrong, birthday girl?" Glenn asked, pulling me into his lap.

I shrugged. I didn't want to bring everyone down. This was a place of happiness, not sadness.

"It's not working for you?"

I shook my head, too tired to even speak.

"Okay." He pulled something out of his pocket. "Happy birthday."

He handed me a bag of about twelve different-colored

pills. I was surprised, and relieved. I didn't know how I was going to pay now that I'd run out of money and left Dad's.

"It's a candy assortment," he said. "But you can save them for later. What I've got for you is something different." He offered me a can of Red Bull.

"Red Bull?" I said, screwing up my face.

"It's laced," he said.

I drank it. I didn't even want to know what was in it. I didn't care. I just wanted not to hurt anymore.

Within twenty minutes it hit me, hard. I don't remember a lot after that until I woke up in Glenn's bed. My ears were ringing so loudly I clapped my hands over them to block out the sound. I sat up with my back against the wall, and with blurred vision looked around me. Glenn was asleep next to me. He was naked like I was and I guess we'd had sex, though I don't remember one second of it.

I was suddenly overwhelmed by panic. It surged through my body. I tried to control it but it was like an electric current. My heart was racing.

I sat rigidly in the bed, my back pushing hard into the wall as I fought to breathe. I was gasping, the way someone with asthma gasps. I couldn't calm down. In my panic my leg, which seemed to have a mind of its own, kicked Glenn hard. He rolled over in his sleep, and the sight of him naked made me want to vomit.

My fingernails dug into the palms of my hands. I couldn't remember last night. The Red Bull, but then nothing. Why couldn't I breathe? Tears streamed down my face. I couldn't get enough air into my lungs. What had happened to me? What had I done? This time I kicked him deliberately and he opened his eyes ever so slightly.

"What the fuck, Mia?" he said, sleepy and annoyed.

"I can't breathe," I gasped at him, clutching at my throat. "Help me."

He rolled back over. And I lost it. I was dying. I couldn't calm down. No one was going to help me. I clawed at my throat. My breath came out in short, jagged puffs. I jumped up off the bed, covered in sweat.

"Glenn!" I screamed at him, but my voice sounded like it was coming from miles away. "Glenn."

"Settle, Mia, you're just G'd out," he muttered angrily.

Was that it? GHB? I was shaking violently. It was like my body was trying to get out of its skin. The ringing in my ears was getting louder. I was going crazy.

I scrabbled around on the filthy floor looking for my clothes. There were used condoms under the bed, empty bottles, porno magazines. I was on my hands and knees, gasping, when from somewhere a rational voice came into my head.

Get a grip, the voice demanded.

I sat on the edge of the bed, clutching my clothes against my naked chest. My heart was still racing, but I was breathing. I'd been breathing the whole time. I took a deep breath and tried to hold it, but it escaped me quickly. I sat trembling and took another one. This time I held it longer. I sat for at least five minutes, watching my chest rise and fall. There were bruises on my legs and a bite mark on my left breast. My forehead, above my left eye, throbbed, and I put a hand to it and winced in pain. There was a lump the size of a tennis ball there. What had I done? The panic welled up again.

Get a grip, the voice said again.

And I listened to it. I sat on the edge of the bed, trembling and breathing. When I thought I had my breathing under control I slowly got dressed. My hands were shaking so badly I couldn't do up my bra, so I stuffed it in my bag. I pulled my T-shirt on, but it was wet and stank of vomit so I shoved that in my bag too. I picked one of Glenn's cigarette-smelling flannel shirts up off the floor. It was way too big, and my fingers were trembling so much I could hardly do up the buttons. I took my time, talking to my fingers over the deafening drone in my ears. I couldn't balance on one leg to get my panties and jeans on, so I sat on the filthy floor of his filthy flat and wriggled into them. I was aching all over. It felt like we'd had sex all night long. I couldn't find my shoes, but I didn't care. As I opened the door he rolled over in his sleep and called my name.

"Go to sleep, Glenn," I said, but I could barely hear my voice over the ringing in my ears.

I picked my way through the sleeping bodies on the living room floor. There were half-naked guys everywhere. I tried not to look around me. The place stank.

Outside it was early morning, and everything felt surreal. The ringing in my ears was getting louder. I couldn't shake it. I walked two blocks to a park and then rifled through my bag. As I sat on the park bench I heard the city waking–doors slamming, engines starting, the cawing of a magpie. I listened to a truck rumble down the street. Stop, hiss, garbage clattered into the back of it, another hiss and the bin touched the ground again. There was one bar left on my cell. I scrolled my phone book and hit Send.

"Mia?" Mom sounded wide awake.

"It's me," I said, and couldn't hold back the wail. "Mom, please come and get me."

When she arrived I was still crying. There was snot on my face and vomit in my hair. All the time I waited for her to come, panic kept threatening to push me over the edge, but that same voice kept telling me to get a grip. It calmed me, but freaked me out too. I didn't want to hear voices in my head. My body felt numb. What had I done to myself?

I was terrified I'd gone insane. I didn't feel like I belonged to my body anymore. I watched as Mom got out of the car, her dressing gown flapping behind her like a cape as she ran toward me. She was still in her pajamas, and her hair was a mess. I sat motionless, watching her like I was outside my body and this was a movie.

"Mia, Mia," she said, stroking the tears off my face.

She put her arms around me without saying anything. She drove, one eye on the road and the other on me. She was very calm. She looked so tired, like I felt. When she got to the driveway she turned the engine off and sat looking at me.

"I think I should take you to the doctor," she said finally.

I nodded. My throat was on fire and everything hurt.

"I need to have a shower," I said, and my voice sounded scratchy and distant. My ears were still ringing loudly.

She helped me out of the car like I was sick and held my

arm as we walked through the door. The house was empty.

"Where's Jord?" I managed to say.

She shook her head, like I shouldn't speak, but said, "It's Dad's weekend."

It didn't make sense. Why was he at Dad's when it was only Friday?

She helped me out of my vile-smelling clothes.

"It's Sunday, Mia," she said.

I tried to work it out. My birthday was on Thursday, so how could it be Sunday? She turned on the tap, adjusted the temperature, and I got into the shower. I watched her looking at my body and I couldn't tell what she was thinking. My legs gave up. I slid down the tiled wall to the floor of the shower. My eyes were open, but I couldn't see. It was raining inside my head. Water ran over my face, into my eyes and mouth. I was drowning in tears and water. Then Mom got in with me, still in her pajamas, and held me under the spray.

sophie

Three days is a long time when you don't know where someone is. Mia had vanished. The cops were useless. Mia was a runaway, but she was also sixteen. She had a place to stay and, as far as anyone knew, wasn't in danger or committing criminal acts. But I knew she was in danger. I knew what Glenn would and could do. The cops said they were investigating and that if they felt she wasn't in the right environment they'd order her home, but of course they had to find her first—and they couldn't find her. Since the last phone call, Mia was mute.

I knocked ineffectually against the tall, thick, solid wood door of Lewis Scott's house until I noticed an intercom system. I pressed the button, self-consciously aware I was probably being watched.

"Hello, Sophie Spencer." Lewis sounded very up.

"Hi," I looked up at the camera. "Can I talk to you?"

"Sure, sure, come in."

The door opened automatically. Everything worked quietly and seamlessly in Lewis's world. I shivered as I walked through his cold house. Through the huge window I saw him sitting with some friends out by the pool.

"What's up?" Lewis asked.

"I'm looking for Glenn."

Lewis laughed. "Straight to the source," he said cryptically.

"I don't know what you mean," I said. "Where does he live? I don't believe you don't know. You're his friend, you must know where he lives."

"I thought you'd know, Sophie Spencer." He got up and mixed a drink. I shook my head when he offered it to me. He was acting like an arrogant pig. "You've been there. Or so I hear."

I curled my fingers tightly into my palms. "Whatever. Where does he live?"

"I told Dominic, I don't know." He shrugged as though colossally bored. "The dealer always comes to you."

The knowledge filled me with horror. How stupid could I be? Glenn was the dealer. Lewis wasn't his friend. I'd been in worse danger than I'd realized. And now Mia was.

"Mia's there, Lewis, and she's in trouble."

For one second Lewis looked like maybe he was concerned. And then it was gone. He shrugged. "She's a big girl. She can look after herself."

And so we waited. We waited for Mia to call. I waited for her mom to tell me she'd heard from her. Every morning I was filled with the same hope. And then on the third day I suddenly considered she might be gone. Gone for good. She could've OD'd. Glenn was a criminal who obviously had no regard for human life. Why would he take care of her? I was sure it was too late. I hated myself for giving up on her, but now I was terrified of her mom calling.

mia

Mom toweled me dry like I was a baby. She went through the clothes in my wardrobe, holding them up and then throwing them on the bed when she saw none of them would fit me. In the end she went downstairs for a steak knife and pushed a hole through an old belt, just so I could keep a pair of pants up.

"You're so thin," she said sadly as she pulled the belt tight.

I just nodded my head at her. She still hadn't asked me anything. I sat on the bed. My old room felt like someone else's. It was so pretty and comfortable. The bed smelled so clean.

Mom picked up my hairbrush and brushed the tangles out of my wet hair. "I've made an appointment with Dr. Herneman. He's coming in to meet us at his office."

I watched her in the mirror, studying me. My hair was past my shoulders and halfway down my back. I didn't know it had got so long. Then I noticed how thin my face was, and the black rings under my eyes, my bloodshot whites, the yellowish lump on my forehead. The skin around my mouth was red and flaking, my lips dry and cracked. No wonder she hadn't asked what I'd been doing. She could see for herself.

In the doctor's office I still felt detached from my body. I sat on the hard plastic chair breathing in the clinical air. Mom sat next to me. Dr. Herneman's been our family doctor since I was born. Mom's taken me to him for every childhood ailment. He knows my complete medical history. When he lifted the back of my shirt to listen to my chest I stared at the floor. He examined the lump on my head, and shone a light in my eyes.

"Do you know how this happened?" he asked.

I shook my head. My neck ached. The last three days were lost to me. I couldn't remember any of it.

He wanted to do tests for pregnancy and sexually transmitted diseases. I was terrified of knowing and equally frightened of not knowing. That voice in my head kept saying, What have you done, Mia? What have you done?

I lay back on the bed, behind the curtain. Mom stayed

in her seat by his desk. He inserted the speculum and I went rigid with pain.

"I think we'll need to do a full internal examination," he said softly.

My eyes were squeezed tightly shut, but tears still escaped. I nodded my head.

Back at his desk Dr. Herneman started making notes on his computer. "We need to fill in an assessment and referral form," he said. "You need to answer me as honestly as you can."

I nodded wordlessly. There seemed no point in lying anymore.

"What drugs have you been using?"

"Mostly ecstasy and weed," I said quietly, without lifting my eyes.

"Anything else?"

"I drank a can with GHB in it."

"What's that?" Mom sounded frightened. "Is that the date rape drug?"

"It's a powerful sedative," the doctor replied. "The difference between getting high and an overdose is almost impossible to determine." I was staring at the carpet and felt them looking at each other. "That's why there have been so many deaths."

Mom made a small oh sound.

"Anything else?" he asked.

I thought of the bag of pills Glenn had given me, but I didn't remember taking any of them. I'd taken the GHB and passed out. Hadn't I?

"Alcohol," I said. "Lots of rum. Maybe cocaine. I don't know about anything else. I actually thought today was Friday." I looked at Mom, who had tears on her cheeks and was wringing the strap of her purse.

"It would seem you had an overdose of GHB," he said. "Obviously not fatal, but enough to render you unconscious, in a comalike state. You show signs of neck snap."

"Of what?"

"An overdose of GHB causes a person to lose consciousness so rapidly their heads often snap forward and hit a surface." He lightly touched the lump on my head. "Like that. How long have you been using?"

I didn't want to say it. Mom looked so scared and old. I felt exhausted. I just shrugged. "Since the start of the year."

"I want to refer you to a psychiatrist," he said, tapping

at his keyboard. "I think we need to admit you to a rehabilitation clinic."

The suggestion was shocking. I looked at Mom, terrified. I didn't want to go into a nuthouse. I didn't want to be labeled psycho. Or druggie. What would happen to me in there?

"Mom?" I said, grabbing her hand. She squeezed mine tightly.

"Does she have to?" Mom asked.

"It's the best chance she's got for recovery," he said.

sophie

At school I had to field all sorts of questions about Mia, and it made me mad how judgmental everyone was. People like Tanisha and Sasha even, asking as though they were so concerned for her welfare. "The poor thing," Sasha said to me, like she really cared, "imagine going into rehab." Because they'd been lucky and got away with it they felt they could look down on her. They made me feel sick—and guilty.

I hadn't seen her, hadn't been to the rehab center. I imagined her locked up in some dark and seedy Cuckoo's Nest with dirty, tiled bathrooms and crazed nurses waving syringes. Dom tried to reassure me. "It won't be like that, Soph. Not the one Mia's in. Dad says it's one of the best."

I went to her house nearly every day. It was like my penance for not doing enough earlier, for turning my back on her when she needed me. I remembered how awful I felt when it seemed she didn't care about me. "She's doing well," Rae told me. "She's starting to face what's happened. We all are."

Days went by at school and gradually interest in Mia faded. It was like the guy who'd OD'd. One minute he was the hot topic of conversation, with everyone trying to outdo each other with what they'd heard, and next thing all the talk was about Wolfmother coming to the Summer Daze Festival next year. Life went on and the casualties faded into the ether. Except for me. I tried writing to Mia. I wanted to put it all on paper, explain it, to myself as well as to her. I wanted her forgiveness. But none of the letters sounded right, so I didn't send them.

mia

I started to have flashes of missing memory. Those three days that had vanished began to reveal themselves to me at night in little snippets. I'd wake in a panic and have to work to calm myself down. I never managed to piece it all together. There are still huge gaps I can't fill, and a part of me doesn't want to, because the parts I do remember are so disgusting.

I remember being half-dressed in Glenn's living room, dancing to the music in front of his friends. I think I'd taken pills from the bag he gave me. And I remember being with two other guys. The memory makes me shudder. I let them treat my body like shit. I was so out of it, I didn't care. Nothing stopped me, not even the physical pain of what they did. I think I drank more GHB, but I'm not sure. I just know that for three days I completely abandoned any sense of self I had.

I was sitting on my bed, writing in my journal–something my counselor encouraged me to do–when she stuck her head around the door. "You've got a visitor," she said. And then I saw Sophie standing behind her.

I swallowed nervously. "Let's go outside," I said, feeling my chest constrict.

We sat under the shade of a huge old tree and I stared at the warped surface of its bark. I didn't know what to say to her. What had Glenn done to her? No wonder she hated me. I shivered.

"Mia, I'm so sorry I turned my back on you," she said eventually.

I couldn't believe she was apologizing to me. "But I'm the one who's sorry."

"I should've told you what happened that night," she said, "but things were so complicated. Lately, I keep thinking that if only I'd told you, maybe things wouldn't have ended up so bad."

But I'd been so involved in myself I hadn't really cared about her problems. And I know it wouldn't have made much difference then, even if she had told me.

Sophie kept talking. "That night we'd gone to his place.

He was going to get his keys and drive me home. He had some friends over." She was looking away from me now. "I remember drinking a rum he gave me and it affected me so badly I could hardly speak. The next thing I knew I woke up on the floor of his bedroom.

"I wasn't sure what he'd done to me. I couldn't remember anything." She brushed tears away. "But I was terrified. I thought …" She was having trouble controlling her voice. "I thought he was going to rape me. I was afraid he was going to kill me."

"You should've told me, you should've made me listen."

"I tried," she sounded defensive, "but you wouldn't."

I couldn't argue with her. I hadn't wanted to hear her; I didn't want her to spoil my fun. "You didn't tell anyone?"

"I told a bit. But … I just wanted to forget about it and try to get on with my life." She shrugged. "There was nothing anyone could do about it anyway."

She was right. I'd been down this road already, talking with a social worker at the center. Glenn couldn't be charged with date rape because GHB leaves the system so quickly. And, aside from a vague memory of sexual assault, girls like Sophie and me are not, apparently, good witnesses.

We sat there quietly for a while. Sophie cupped her face

in her hands and stared off into space. I guess the whole situation was weird for both of us. We knew each other so well, but we didn't know how to act around each other anymore.

"So, what do you do around here?" she said to break the silence.

I waved a hand in the air. "You know, the usual detox kind of stuff. Prescription drugs and therapy with Freud." I put on an exaggerated German accent. "Ve haf vayz of making you zink."

And then she laughed, a deep, strong laugh. Suddenly it was easy. It was Soph and me again. We sat in the sunshine of the rehab center laughing and talking, not about what had happened, but other things, the fun things we used to do.

ACKNOWLEDGMENTS

My thanks go to the usual suspects, my family and friends, for their constant support and encouragement. Thanks to my students and colleagues at St. Stephen's School Carramar who have to answer my questions and listen to my progress reports. I'd like to thank everyone at Fremantle Press, but particularly Janet for helping discover Sophie, and Cate for her unwavering dedication and time. For this North American version my big love goes to Pip Squeak—thank you Jennifer Phillips, for so many things. Thank you to Annick Press for giving me a voice internationally. And thank you to all the people who have shared their stories with me.

FURTHER INFORMATION AND ADVICE

Online:

teens.drugabuse.gov

nineline.org

www.addict-help.com

www.checkyourself.com

www.focusas.com

www.phoenixhouse.org

www.freevibe.com

www.talktofrank.com

www.na.org/pdf/litfiles/us_english/IP/EN3113_2008.pdf

In the United States:

Covenant House Nineline: 1-800-999-9999
Free 24-hour telephone line. Services available in English and Spanish.

Counselors can also respond to your concerns online at: nineline.org. Click on the "email the Nineline" link.

National Drug and Alcohol Treatment Referral Service: 1-800-662-HELP
Call for referrals to treatment programs.

Substance Abuse & Mental Health Services Administrator: To locate a treatment program near you, try the Substance Abuse Treatment Facility Locator at findtreatment.samhsa.gov. Click on your state on the map, and enter the name of your city and state in the search engine. You can include your address and search for programs from 1 to 100 miles from the location entered.

Narcotics Anonymous: To locate a number to call, go to www.na.org and click on "helplines," then the "Phonelines Table of Contents" link. From there, you can click in your area, click on your country, then your state or province, and finally city. You can also email them at: FSTeam@na.org or call: (818) 773-9999 and ask for fellowship services.

In Canada:

Kids Help Phone: 1-800-668-6868
Free 24-hour telephone line. Services available in French and English.

You can also visit their website to post a question to a counselor by entering the "kids site" at www.kidshelpphone.ca/. Click on the "Get Counselling" tab, then the "Ask a Counsellor" tab.

Canadian Centre on Substance Abuse has a list of telephone numbers for information on where to go for treatment in your province or territory. Many of the phone lines are answered 24 hours a day. Go to www.ccsa.ca/ and click on the "Topics" tab, and choose "Treatment."

First Nations and Inuit Health Branch (FNIHB) has a Treatment Centre Directory of all native in-patient treatment centers. You can search by region. Go to www.hc-sc.gc.ca/, click on the "First Nations, Inuit & Aboriginal Health" tab, then click on "NNADAP Treatment Centres" tab and finally the "Treatment Centres by Region" link.

ABOUT THE AUTHOR

Kate McCaffrey grew up in Perth, Western Australia. She has a degree in English and art and a diploma in education. She lives in Mariginiup, Western Australia, with her partner, their two daughters, two dogs, a cat, and a rabbit.

Her first novel, *Destroying Avalon*, was published in Australia in 2006. It won the Western Australian Young Readers' Book Award for older readers, the Western Australian Premier's Book Award for Young Adults, was a notable book in the Children's Book Council of Australia Book Awards, and was highly commended in the Australian Family Therapists Children's Literature Awards.

You can find more information about Kate and her work at www.katemccaffrey.com